TEARS OF LOVE

SHAMS-I TABRIZI

A Biographical Novel

TEARS OF LOVE

SHAMS-I TABRIZI - A Biographical Novel

Sinan Yagmur

KARATAY AKADEMI PUBLISHING – 2011

Non Fiction – 1

Editor In Chief

Mustafa Kemal Avcioglu

Editor

Hikmet Yilmaz

English Translation

Nurullah Koltas

Proofreading

Saliha Han Simsek

Cover Photograph

Salih Arikan

Cover Design

masske.com

First edition

July 2011, Konya

ISBN: 978-605-113-049-1

Karatay Akademi Publishing

Fevzi Cakmak Mahallesi Menemen Sk. No: 34

Phone: 0332. 342 5844 Fax: 0332. 342 5845

www.karatayakademi.com

Karatay / Konya

Print and Cover

Dizgi Ofset

Yeni Matbaacılar Sit. Dizgi Cd. No:6

Karatay/KONYA/TURKEY

Phone: 0332. 342 00 05 - 342 07 42

TEARS OF LOVE

SHAMS-I TABRIZI

A Biographical Novel

By

Sinan Yagmur

Translated by

Nurullah Koltas

Karatay akademi

PUBLISHER'S FOREWORD

One of the most important elements that constitute a nation is the culture. The nations those convey both material and spiritual elements to the future generations successfully can strengthen and develop their national awareness. Given the fact that Turkish culture and civilization are based on the values and love for humanity, our publishing house took over some crucial responsibilities concerning the issue in question. The thought of Rumi, who loved humanity by means of a profound tolerance and compassion only for the fact that one is human, attracted many seekers of truth all around the world. There are approximately 200 books written on his way and thought in the USA.

"Rumi is a man of love who added an eternal substance in the very essence of these lands; He is the sound of mercy." In this era in which we suffer, we need Rumi's voice more than before in order to remove the seeds of hatred and enmity, conflicts, tensions and polarizations. Thus, we established Karatay Akademi Yayinlari in 2010 to unite our hearts for this purpose and to convey the message of love and affection to humanity. Within the framework of this mission, we tried to introduce the life of Shams al-Tabrizi who discovered Rumi and made him ripen as a biographical novel. We will continue to introduce new titles to the readers on the same line of thought.

SINAN YAGMUR

He was born in 1965 in Nevsehir where *Hunkar Haji Bektash* had left a spiritual influence. He graduated from primary and secondary schools in Kirsehir, a city sanctified by Ahi Awran Wali. Under the influence of a sign in one of his dreams, Sinan Yagmur went to the home of Pîr Mawlana, which is also the home of love. In 1985, he could not resist the voice of his heart and he touched the fire in Tannura. Then he blew *Tannura and Fire* line by line as his first book. He heard the voice of Shams, the martyr of love. He was petrified by astonishment and stopped. He resolved letter by letter... he wrote for the ones whose eyes were dazzled by sunlight not to take refuge in shadows. He collected the *Tears of Love* in order to move love from the streets to the pages. These pages, which moisten the flames, address the sun so that it may flow in your hearts as dews:

"If rivers had dried up, there would not be any oceans. If love had not been esteemed, then Adam and Eve would not have been created by the one that knows you better than yourself."

Many thanks to Ms. Nazan Bekiroglu who possesses the meaning and who has great courage to write Shams "as he is".

FOREWORD

Shams: I address the writers who have not written the truth so far! The writers today cannot write without borrowing from the real writers who lived before them. However, they think that what they wrote would be readable only then. They are like the moon and they do not possess their own light… and their own Shams (sun)!

I do not know why they fear to interact with the main source. They think what if they were stricken by that light; what if their eyes were dazzled by that very light; what if all they thought they knew were not true… What if all they wrote was mere illusion….

How can one attain the truth while living in false lives? How can a sound, a world come to your pen?… You would then appeal to those real writings written and lived before you… and you attempt to write concerning those who fulfilled that troublesome journey instead of establishing a direct relation with the truth; you attempt to write as you reduced the truth by your every false word. How can one who attempts to write on my life convey my ocean to his deserts without knowing me?

To what extent can those who did not experience Sufism and who did not pay a visit to Konya understand me? How dare those who conveyed their false dreams which do not belong to me use my name? The writings hurt my soul more than the strokes of swords. I am Shams who came to destroy the established rules and who rejected the worldly things; then how can they explain me in a wrongly? Why do they place me at the center of their intrigues?

It was necessary to experience love platonically. I did not know that to love someone, to submit yourself to a love madly to experience the beauty, corresponded to grief. I realized that I missed many important things in life… Either I came early or you are late for attainment.

Jamshid abandoned his throne for his beloved whom he saw in his dream but did not know whether that beloved existed or not; and he travelled every inch of Anatolia. I also abandoned my future for Mawlana. Which words can unveil the secrets of Kimya that they dare to write on my Kimya? Whose voice of conscience is it to establish my name and my admirers in their scenario of love? How can these poor people; who fear the deeply rooted plane tree of love and who carry pens that are weak as candle lights, explain me who carries the fire in his hands and the love that becomes a plane tree?

Fire (love), tree, water are only words for you… you immediately begin to make a story and try to place these words in it… you never wonder their inner realities…the inner sounds of words… their wing beats, and their participation into the harmonious invocation of the universe. You cannot see how they transformed you while living… you are only interested in stories… you try to force words to penetrate into those awkward stories as you do not have any life story… this is a kind of fait accompli writing! You do not know how to console the words! How would you feel whom you are without feeling the spirit given to them? Can a man touch a word without knowing love? How can he put it into writing?.. How can you plant that tree without preparing the garden?... Soil is required for the fertile garden of writing…

Love is required to hail light above your garden of writing … is it possible for a garden, soil or water to exist; or a single word without knowing it? Can one attempt to write without knowing love?

A Unique Introduction for Shams

Shams is the one who made Mawlana as he is. Mawlana used to be only a scholar until he met Shams. He was admired by people of Konya and was a ripen and reasonable teacher at madrasa. It was Shams who made an ecstatic out of a reasonable Muslim scholar who was confined within intellect and science that emerged from intellect.

Shams came all of a sudden, at a time, which Mawlana did not expect or hope at the age of forty. However, this age is a prophetic one. Moreover, it is the eleventh hour.

The door was knocked and it was wide open. The traveler entered silently. He was a passerby… he only called upon … but stayed there..

Shams was a stranger. This proud man who came unexpectedly is proud with a completely different pride. He regards false humbleness as arrogance and thus hates it. If capability is innate, then he is proud thinking that to hide is also falsification. That's why his tongue is sharp as such. He is beyond common rules but marvelous as well. Furthermore, there is an invitation to "trouble" in each of his words.

A stranger of darkness and black; a traveller that misleads; the beloved that keeps the traveler away from his destination.

His identity is obscure but this is not of great importance: the hair of Shams is the night of Tabriz. And his face is the sun of Isfahan. *mahr* and *mah* emerge from his words. For, Shams admonishes people. A great meeting takes place in eternity.

He was Shams. Shams means "the sun" in Persian. He caused such an overflowing that the tides of Mawlana, which are like vast seas but formed by the Moon on small seas and in tranquil and safe soul that has not seen any winds, is almost nothing compared with this overflowing of Shams. For,

Mawlana is an ocean. He has followed moons and seas but now is taken by the attraction of the sun.

They meet just as the meeting of two seas rather than the meeting of water with soil in a manner different from the turmoil of daily life. Shams becomes both the lover and the beloved of Mawlana; the seeker and the spiritual Guide. In fact, the overflow of abundance lies in this multiplicity. It is not certain who the lover is and who the beloved is in this meeting. What a grief! This is love; one that has already transcended the confines of space, time and gender reached the very source of love via this transcendence and one, which is impossible to be conceived by this insolent sight. The ones who do not understand are excused due to their lack of understanding. How is that they may conceive it?..

Perhaps due to his entirely blooded future, Shams divided Mawlana's life into two equal parts like a knife. Mawlana was not the same as he used to be. He gave up self-possession if he was as such and he went beyond the limits of intellect unlike his past.

Shams was not silence. Then how did Mawlana bear such turmoil? How is it that he remained unburnt despite burning?

For sure, the apparent character of Shams was his darkness. However, his darkness is luminous because of being secret rather than darkness. Although his identity, family, lineage and nature are uncertain, Shams is still the best name that corresponds with this marvelous darkness. Shams… As we stated before, means the sun. Maybe that's why the color of Mawlawi rite is black at the beginning and the white *tannure* (a white and large garment worn by Mawlawis during the *sama*-t.n) opens afterwards.

Name: Mohammed

Father's name: Ali

Homeland: Tabriz

That's all. Nothing more. I hope this will go on as such. For, there is no need for any extra information. What a sentimental speech it is. And it suits Shams very well.

There are two well-known domes in Islamic world: both of them are green: *qubba al-hadra*. One belongs to the Holy Prophet (P.B.U.H) and the other one belongs to Mawlana. Mawlana is under his own green Dome among his father and son, his *Chalabi* and scribe, *Salah al-Din* and *Husam al- Din,* and those gentle ones who cared for him much. He was a rose so noble not to be touched; he was delicate in his delicateness. He was dignified in his dignity. He was a townsman, so refined in his elegance and graciousness. Shams was far away… in his darkness… in a corner… in his solitude. He lies there alone.

Loneliness is the representation of love. Death is compensation of love

Each love is compensated by a head.

It was Shams who sacrificed his head as compensation this time.

(Nazan Bekiroglu/Cumle Kapisi)

Though everything is submitted to man
Man became a burden for himself

MY FAMILY

I am Mohammad, son of Ali; or as they called me throughout history, Shams-i Tabrizi. My grandfather is an Azeri Turk. My father is Ali the Melekdadoglu.

My granddad was from Khorasan. He grew up in Alamut and became a disciple of Hasan Sabbah. Due to an economical enmity, my family migrated to Khorasan and settled thereof. I was born there in 1183. They named me Mohammad. My ancestors accepted *Ismailiyya* a branch of *Shia* and accepted the *Jafariyya* School of Jurisprudence. My grandfather is said to be an ill-tempered and sharp-tongued man. Because of my quarrelsome and outspoken nature during my childhood, my mother used to liken me to my grandfather whom I never saw. I could not endure the hypocrite nature of people. I would criticize people when I saw those committing wrong deeds. As a result of such a characteristic, my dad would say:

- Your grandfather put us in trouble by means of his sharp tongue. We had to move here, because he could not get along with anyone there. You should at least know how to control your words.

My father sent me to a *madrasa* in order to become well behaved and to be educated through studying Holy Quran. At the age of seven, I started memorizing the verses of our Holy Book although my peers could not utter even a simple sentence. The hodja there named me "*Skylark*" since I was skinny and frail. However, at first I would become a falcon and then a turtledove, but they had no idea about this process.

My classmates could not complete even their initial phase (in classical Arabic classes in *madrasa*s, students begin having a preparatory education before reading the Quran. This process includes learning the alphabet and some simple phrases. And these exercises are combined in a small booklet called "*juz*"-t.n.) within a whole month. I began reading the Quran the very day I arrived there. My teacher was surprised and said: "you are not normal, oh Skylark". That night, my father woke up for the night prayer (*tahajjud*). I made ablution (*wudu*) and began praying behind him. After the *salam* (the last part concludes the canonical prayer-t.n.) He said:

- Son! The night prayer is not one that is performed in congregation. It is preferred after waking up at night. Moreover, you are not at an age to be responsible for it. Yet, I am pleased to see you praying. He kissed my cheeks and went into his bedroom.

I took the Quran from its lectern (rahla) and began reciting it. I managed to finish reciting the entire Quran by the rise of the morning sun. I was drowsy. I almost fell asleep as I was lying on the sofa. The Angels were reciting verses in my dream. I woke up… I closed the Holy Book with an ineffable joy after waking up. I realized that I memorized some verses I recited so as not to forget them. When I opened a page randomly, I saw that it was the *sura* (one of the 114 sections in Quran) of *al-Shams* (the Sun). As I went on reciting, I came to the 10th verse and felt as if my chest swelled out like a balloon. I fainted there. When I regained consciousness, my fingers still were on the 10th verse, "truly he succeeds that purifies it, and he feels that corrupts it (one's self)". I was taken by this verse. I could not move; I was raptured so deeply that I fell in love with this *sura*. Everyone understands the "purification" in this verse as cultivation of the self. However, ripening the self means also the stumbling of Satan. Just as the seed is sown in the soil, the self is purified from unknown materials; thus it is purified via divinely hopes and submits itself to divine Grace and Bliss. The following morning I told my parents:

- Call me *Shams* from now on. Your son fell in love with the *sura al-Shams*.

From that day on my name began to be known as Shams. I came to be known as *Shams-i Tabrizi* (Shams of Tabriz) after my birthplace. My teacher of religious sciences, *Ruqn al-Din Sajasi*, began calling me as *paranda*, which means one who flies; as, I used to rush into the garden during boring lessons. He was right in calling me as such. It is possible that he felt I would be a *Shams-i Paranda* (the flying *Shams*) who would fly from one place to another without being dependent on anything through my entire life.

My teachers were *Abu Bakr Salabaf*, *Shaykh Kermani* and *Ruqn al-Din Sajasi*. Nevertheless, the style of my lessons was question and answer rather than being merely teaching. Our circle of learning generally consisted of debates. The only master who would satisfy my soul was *Mawlana Jalal al-Din*. A *Hodja* should not only be a teacher but also a student. He should not say, "I will speak and you will listen". You should understand without speaking. You should share the things in your heart; you should not speak as if giving sermon on a pulpit and pose an encumbrance on your heart. He should sometimes mold the meaning and utter a single word so as to flow meaning included in many volumes of books. A teacher as such should present an ocean within a single drop. He should be the seeker and one who is sought. He should be one who devote himself and go out of the routine. He should not be reticent.

MY CHILDHOOD

You are an animal from the point of your body
And an angel at soul
Thus, You will appeal both to Heaven and earth.

I experienced a strange state (*hâl* in Arabic-t.n.) during my childhood. I would sleep at night and eat nothing from morning until evening. However, I would feel neither restlessness nor hunger. It was as if a hidden hand kept me standing strongly. My mother would bring fresh bread, pizzas, and also some meat and desserts. When I had even a morsel of them I would not swallow it. There were days in which I lived without eating and drinking. My peers would play games but I would sit under a tree from morning to evening. As my father told, I was talking to unseen beings in delirium. I could not understand that state, nor did anyone else. Even my father did not know what happened to me. He said:

- You are not a madman, then what's the reason for this state? You do not possess ripeness and piety required on this path. Your mother and aunt are sad for your present condition. They think that it is genies which caused all this. They wanted me to take you to shrines and have spiritual people heal you. I told them to be silent and said that you were not mad. Oh, Mohammad! What's the matter with you?

I told my father:

- Listen to me from my own words... You and I are in such a state that it is as if they put a goose egg under a hen. Then a baby goose came out of the eggs. It grew up and came nearby a River. It suddenly jumped into the river. The mother hen fluttered around it. However, she was poultry and thus she could not jump into the water. Our situation is just the same. Oh father! I see an ocean to swim in. My home is that ocean and my state is just like that of a seafowl. If you're like me, come then. However, I'm not like you in this ocean. Go and mix with other poultry.

I think these profound sentences made my father anxious. He said:

- If you treat your friends as such, then how would you treat your enemies?

I would turn my face even when they mentioned food. I sometimes took the food they gave me only to be courteous and gave it to the children playing in the street. This coquetry was for my dad. For instance, one day our cat spilt milk and broke the bowl. My father did not utter a single word to the cat and was not angry with me. He smiled and said, "What have you done this time? At least by this we have probably had a narrow escape from some greater trouble. The Almighty bestowed His Mercy and we were saved."

It was these words that spoiled my appetite. I could not eat anything within those 3-4 days. I feared not only from public but also from the All-Truth. I ceased to eat or drink with no reason. When my father told me to eat or drink, I would answer, "I cannot do that". I became so weak that I could have flown out of the window like a bird. They said, "There is a mystery in it, but it does not unveil its mystery to you."

There was a madman (*majdhub* is not an ordinary madman but one who turns to be an ecstatic out of divine love-t.n.)

who would talk about secrets. They used to keep him indoors in order to test his abilities. However, he somehow found ways to go out. One day while my father was scolding me, this man came towards us, raised his fist at my father and pointing at me. He said:

-Are you bothering this child? If so, I'll throw you into that river.

The river was flowing towards Lake *Tur* and had enough power to wash an enormous elephant away. Then the madman turned to me and greeted me with full respect. Finally, he left us.

I would not perform my supererogatory prayers within my father's presence. How could I show my inward state and world? He was a well-charactered man and possessed nobility. He would utter a few words and then burst into tears. But he was not a lover; being a man with good character is one thing and being a lover is another.

I would not allow anyone to die without me. When I heard that someone is dying, I would rush there. If I disappeared for a few hours, then my family members would say, "look for someone who is almost dying; Shams must be there". I would watch this journey.. It is necessary to observe death before you die. It was only for this reason that I would open the cover of the coffin in the nearby masjid's *ghasilhana* (a place where dead bodies are washed and prepared to be buried according to Islamic funeral rituals). I would lay down in it and try to feel death until morning. I never slept in wool or cotton beds. I would sleep either on pure wood or on rocks, under a tree or even in a coffin. When I went to hostels or caravanserais, I would put the rugs and carpets aside and sleep on straw mats. I never slept more than four hours that was in cessations of an hour. There is no single night in which I have not prayed the night prayer.

YOUTH

The youth has four principles: the smell of homeland, the smell of books, the smell of your children and the smell of the Beloved one.

I wasn't yet an adolescent. When my father gave me under supervision of a *hodja*. I saw him whispering in the hodja's ears. I began smiling. What could force me to stay here: either I would run away or they would go mad. The students, who mimed the teacher's lips like parrots, really annoyed me. I remained silent when he asked any questions.

One day, the hodja told a parable to a student as he was holding an apple in his hand. "I saw Allah and wanted an apple from Him. He gave it to me. Abu Yazid (*Bistami*) wanted Allah from Himself and even he wanted another person in another one. Who would you want, my son? "The student said, "I would also wish Allah from Himself as a respect for Abu Yazid (or *Bûyazid* in some old texts – t.n). He asked the same question to me and I replied, "I'd rather wish you". He lowered his head and nodded but told nothing. I also did not say anything; but words, phrases and meanings began overflowing in my heart. Some strange state (*hâl*) which would have never been experienced by any child took me away. Then the hodja advised my father to send me to a *madrasa* in Damascus in order to crown my education. My father kept his advice and decided to send me to Damascus. He prayed for me before leaving:

- May Allah give you a friend each day to manifest the knowledge and truths of ancients and also those of the forthcoming ones. May the rivers of wisdom flow into your heart from his tongue and may that wisdom be embodied in letters and sounds. The title of that embodiment would be named under your name.

My extraordinary features compared with those of that period, my personality that surprised the person I addressed through my words, my rebellion nature against the valid taboos and customs caused either reactions or interests of people around. People defined me as an unbearable and weird person when they heard my harsh words and interpretations. I did not care about their thoughts.

I was in a caravanserai in Damascus. A man asked:

- Aren't you coming to the *takka* (a place where dervishes come together and perform the rites of their order)?
- I do not deserve going there.
- How about going to a madrasa?

I said:

- I am not one of those who debate. Even though I conceive the words, it does not behoove me to debate or discuss. For, if I speak via my tongue, they would laugh. They would call me a heretic and accuse me of heresy. I am strange and caravanserais are the places for strange ones.

I have a custom of asking people near me: "Sir! Will you speak or listen?" If he says, "I will speak", I may listen to him continuously for three days so that he might go away and I might get rid of him. If he says, "I will listen", I tell him that it is possible to get along with him. I begin speaking and he might speak during the conversation:

There is a certain man who is speaking in a sorrowful voice in this end of the world of qualities and quantities! His eyes are even sharper than those of eagles! His face is the witness of the inward fire the burning of which increases gradually! He is made of a passionate soul and burning soil. The physicians who were deprived of love and ecstasy submitted his heart to a doctor to be cured.

I entered a counsel of friends in Damascus. A certain Shaykh was explaining the extinction in God (*fana*) to his disciples. I rushed in anger:

- Where do you see Allah?
- The faces of beautiful ones are like mirrors. I see Him on those mirrors.
- Then?
- I see Him in water and soil.
- Go away you idiot. Since you see Allah in the mirror of water and soil, and see me in the mirror of another, then why don't you look in the mirror of the heart and soul? When I said all these, the disciples thought that these words belonged to a madman and were ready to pounce on me. In the meantime, the shaykh who was sitting on a cotton mat ran towards me and bowed before me:
- May Allah be pleased with you. Although he begged me to stay in his *dargah* (the lodge where the shaykh and his initiates reside-t.n.), I did not pay any attention and left there.

I became a disciple of *Ruqn al-Din Sajasi*, the most renowned sufi master in Damascus; I had no hope whether he could calm down the hurricane within me. I came across him at the *shadirwan* (a kind of fountain where people perform ablution-t.n.). I said:

- Oh Master, what does 'love' mean?
- They borrowed the first cup of wine from the intoxicated sight of *Saqi* (the cupbearer-t.n) they combined all the grief in the world and called them "love".
- Then who transforms the bitter fountain of love into honey?

- Son! Do not seek that ocean of honey here. Go to Konya and you will find it there.
- Where in Konya?
- In the master (*pir*) of love. He is such a master that you will be the one who would ripen him.
- How should I find him? What is his mark or sign?
- He will find you. A caravan will come to Damascus. Greet it. Ask all the caravans. Your beloved one is he who seeks for love in books and seclusion in paths. The devotion for love would determine who sought whom and who found whom.

I travelled from one country to another and one city to another. I went to Pakistan, Azerbaijan, India, China, etc.; no country attracted me. I travelled in Iran, Iraq, and Syria and finally to Holy Lands like a migratory bird (to Mecca and Medina where you can feel the light of Mohammed). I prayed: "Oh, Lord! May Thou bestow me the honor of meeting a spiritual Master (*murshid*) who would increase the fire of love". During my visit to the tomb of the greatest spiritual Guide, our Prophet, "I happened to experience a strange state (*hal*). I fainted.

In my dream, they told me that it is the *Rûm* lands (i.e. Anatolia; Mawlana Jalaleddin is called "Rûmi", Mawlana the Anatolian, in that he lived in Anatolia–t.n) that you seek. I woke up. After performing *Haj* (the circumambulation of Kaba-t.n), I returned to Damascus. There was a hidden talisman that kept me in Damascus. It was as if the Arafat of one whom I look for or the Arafat of whom seeks for me was the streets of Damascus. Arafat means the meeting point. Adam and Eve looked for each other for a month after being sent from Heaven and met on Arafat Hill. Arafat means attainment. "When is my Arafat, oh Lord?"

Before meeting with Mawlana, the reason for travelling from one land to another was the search for a spiritual master. I would ask the shaykhs questions on being devoted to love. I did not show my devotion as I never found what I sought in them. The search for love would lead me to Konya. Neither me nor my beloved understood if I was the seeker or one who is sought?.. I am wondering around, oh love. I am wondering and searching. I am in search of the distant one inside me, oh love! The near far away or the love nearby. I am in search of the inward, oh love. The near inside me is you; you, whom I sought. I seek me, inside you and you inside me, neither in you nor in me or both in you and me; a submission, a peace, an acceptance, a sacrifice and extinction… Yes, I am in search of it, oh love!; a burning in love, a whirling in love, a hearing in love, a feeling in love, a dying in love…

I seek… the nearness inside me
My inward nearby, thee inside me.
I continuously wonder, oh love
Wondering ceaselessly.

I have a fire inside me, oh love, a fire in my heart. I have tears in my eyes, my heart is on fire and my eyes are rivers. I seek, oh love, in the fire inside me, I search for Ibrahim whom fire never burns. I get wet under the waterfall of tears. Neither that fire nor those tears clean my heart. "Do not spill water, oh eye, over the fire in my heart!"

Oh love, I wish you knew of the idols that existed in my house. You say, "The sultan cannot be allowed into the palace unless it is not cultivated" oh Ibrahim, I can hear that. But which sacrifice can purify us of love? Which *ram* can do it? I am in search of purification, cleanliness. As you know, I need love.

What a fire I have in my house of love! I need an Abraham who was a friend of fire. I search, oh love, a path that would make me come closer, a "*buraq*" (a spiritual horse that is believed to take Holy Prophet to the Heaven during his

Nocturnal Journey- t.n) that makes near nearer, perhaps an ascension, a rising upwards, perhaps a hope, an elixir.

I am wondering, oh love, wondering around. I keep running around, oh love! I am a vagabond or maybe a ruined: however, I go on searching. Oh love, I am in search of Noah's saving ark on Mount *Qaf* (an imaginary mountain between *jabulsa* and *jabulqa* or between the east of the east and west of the west – t.n), I passed by all mountains and oceans of fire by devoutness and great zeal; I am in search of Noah to attain the shore of salvation. I am wandering here and there. It is as if I am a vagabond. However, my heart is open to my inward, to the inward sky. I share my feelings with *Anqa* (an imaginary bird that lives on Mount *Qaf*; phoenix –t.n) and communicate with all creatures in Salomon's language.

I am looking for a friend, oh love, for a friend. A friend that comes nearer by sacrifice… A friend that is brought nearer by sacrifice!

A friend is a breath, which revivifies the dead souls. The friend is *Khalil* (the title of Prophet Abraham, which means the Friend of God), the Friend is Jesus, the friend is the pride of universe, the mercy for universe and his grace is the *Habib* (the title of Prophet Mohammed that means the Beloved of God) of the All-Truth.

I seek the Friend of Love!

I am in search of the Perfect Man (*Insan al-Kamil*) a perfect spiritual master. I need a purified shaykh who is like a Companion of the Prophet Mohammed. As a matter of fact, I see faults in those whom I meet as shaykhs. A certain man even claimed that he spoke in the language of the All Truth despite his early age. How can one, whose birth was given by a lady, claim that "he is the language of All Truth? Most of those shaykhs are the bandits of the Religion of Mohammed. It is possible that you will think, "How arrogant and severe

Shams is" as I express my thirst on my search. You will understand me when I find what I searched for

I left those sheikhs who sought profit and glitter. I have never initiated to a sheikh until I met *Mawlana* (lit. our Lord or Master: it is one of Rumi's titles – t.n), I understood that he is a valuable pearl whereas Muhyiddin is only a pebble.

Neither Mawlana nor I attained divine love through humanly love from the eyes of a beautiful girl.. My attainment of true love did not come into existence after human love like those in legends and tales.

[illegible] the [illegible] of the [illegible]

[illegible]

[illegible]

Each man has a certain time for loving,
And one for dying.
But there is no end for me; it is I who am the love
Before which angels prostrated.

I used to liken myself to Hajjaj Yusuf in saying what I thought without any fear; to Abu *Dhar al-Ghiffari* in enduring injustice; to Caliph Omer in maintaining justice. For me, the world full of justice is greater than the one full of mercy.

I used to speak slowly and softly with people. I preferred behaving as Hajjaj did before crowds. I admired his well-known *Qufa* speech. Yusuf Hajjaj demanded to be the governor of city of Qufa. Everyone trembled because of the way he spoke; no one saw him smiling; he was scowling and walking in a gallant manner. The caliph did not want to assign him as a governor; on the other hand, the circumstances in Qufa required a firm governor. All governors left the city even before spending a single month there. Qufa means disorder, mischief making and treachery. They betrayed Caliph Ali and submitted Husayn, the grandson of Holy Prophet, to Yazid the oppressor. They gave their guest "Muslim" to oppressors willingly. Qufa was arrogant and it was full of caprice so as not to understand gentle words and the existing circumstances.

Although Yusuf Hajjaj knew all these very well, he went to Qufa, which everyone feared. He had worn out garments and veiled his face as a beggar. He directly went to the masjid for

Morning Prayer. On the way to masjid, he threw pebbles at the doors and windows to wake them up. The public gathered at the mosque in order to punish him. Almost all the men were there. They wondered about the real intention of this stranger. Who was that huge madman sitting at the pulpit? Why did he throw pebbles at their windows and woke them up? The mysterious man unveiled his face and they trembled with fear. It was Yusuf Hajjaj. On the other hand, he was remembered as Hajjaj the oppressor that was quite contrary to reality. For me, he was a scholar rather than an oppressor. As I said before, justice precedes everything. What goodness has mercy got if is merely a motto?

I admired his speech in Qufa Mosque when I was young. It was as follows:

- I am a famous man. Every glory and action of mine adds to my fame day by day. Let me take my turban off and see who I am. Now, did you see me clearly? Did you recognize me? I see some of you leaning forward to see me better. These necks can be slaughtered very well. I am good at cutting the heads off. I can imagine the blood coming out of those heads cut off.

The leader of the believers emptied his quiver. He chose the sharpest and firmest arrow made of the strongest wood. I am that arrow. Oh, Iraqis! Oh rebels who know nothing more than rebellion and betrayal! Oh, evil-minded people. I am not a mild hearted one who is like soft mold. You who deserve whips and you sons of slaves! I am Hajjaj b. Yusuf. You will see that I never spend my time by threatening people but fulfill the things I say immediately. I hate wasting time and speaking too much. I don't want to see groups of people anywhere. Meetings and assemblies are forbidden for you all! I don't want you to talk secretly. No one should ask each other questions such as "What's going on? What's new? etc. What happens should not interest you, oh sons of incitement!

No one should interfere with any other one's work. Pity for those who are brought to my court! You will walk straightly and never turn your head to any other direction. You will obey the officials I assigned and pledge allegiance to them (*biat*). You will set off only after the pledge of loyalty and obedience. I am angry with politics and gossiping. When I was young, *Sabbahi*s (or they are called "*Hashashis*". They were followers of Hasan Sabbah. Some people believe that the word "Assassin" is derived from their name – t.n) *Malamis*, servants at palaces, they all tried to persuade me for their politics. But it was in vain. Sabbahis threatened me by sending assassins due to their enmity. For, I rejected their policy. I did not take them seriously. I said, "This Shams died before he died". I also hated the policy and invasions of Mongols. Politics is the water of Satan. If you even touch that water to clean yourself, your entire body becomes occupied by the Devil.

Neither did I like writing nor did I allow another to write. I would speak spontaneously and never ceased to speak whatever I thought. I would raise my voice unexpectedly and surprise the audience there. Mawlana was also surprised with my style of speaking and attitude towards people. He asked:

- Oh my *Paranda* (the flying one)! You are so kind to me and to lovers; however, you are frightening and ill-tempered towards others. What's the reason for this?
- I treat those who supplicate sincerely in a humble manner; but I am arrogant and harsh towards the rest. I don't care whether they are sultans or *beg*s.

The sign of those who participate in my circle is that I trust myself so as to be able to say that "the speech of others is bitter and cold for that very person." I never change my attitude. I proclaim the truth. I don't care whether he is offended or not. He who is not loyal to himself cannot be loyal to anyone.

My first advice to Mawlana was to be deaf against others in order to unveil the inner understanding.

I was never attracted by the attraction of the visible world. Is it possible to remain firm if you fear what people say or think? I hate formalism. It is my noble characteristic to exert opposition towards the belief and the thoughts of those who are dependent on mere appearance. Thus, I make their hopes and expectations fruitless and destroy their dreams. I observed all important centers in Islamic countries and entered into the circles of many spiritual leaders in those lands. I have not seen anyone to make me intoxicated as Mawlana did.

I have the habit of asking the person who sits next to me: "Sir! Will you speak or listen?" If he says "I will speak", I may listen to him continuously for three days so that he might go away and I might get rid of him. If he says "I will listen", I tell him that it is possible to get along with him. I begin speaking and he might speak during the conversation.

I have the richness of recognizing the reaction of my addressee beforehand and understand his character and personality by means of the inspiration Allah bestowed upon me. As I regard fame a catastrophe, I veil myself sometimes in a manner and appearance of a merchant. I hate being respected excessively. "I follow the way of Moses in speaking and being in God's intimacy; and of Jesus in abstaining from everything. I constantly observe and spend my time in spiritual seclusion (*uzlah*); those bewildered ones expected miracles from me. I would sense their intentions. However, it is I who reject the miracles exerted out of showing off and for the sake of fame. Showing miracles for the sake of love is all right but trying to show miracles only to please the public is adulatory.

My soul sometimes shakes your selves. I am like a mirror that proclaims your faults, imperfectness and ugliness. That the exoteric people regard me as a simple esoteric shows an underestimation. I ask the following question: "My work, Mawlana is obvious. How about yours?"

"Think of a sheet of paper; one side looks at you and the other side looks at the beloved or each side is directed to another one. You can read the side looking at you but more importantly you should be able to read the side that is turned towards the real friend, the beloved."

It has been ages since I left books. I read hundreds of volumes. Those, which I read, would be stored in my memory. Allah bestowed this ability upon me. I would learn in a single night what is learnt by others in an entire month. I discovered everything on Interpretation of Quran, sayings of Prophet, Jurisprudence, and history of religions, history of Islam, theology and Sufism. I did not like theology at all; I would prefer the faith of a miner to that of a theologian. I completed *balaghat* (rhetoric –t.n) of Arabic and Indian literature when I was just an adolescent. When the hodjas were not aware of the matters in their own manuscripts, I would remind them of their own words. I was just as a walking library. I soon realized that the books did not include what I sought. I reminded this fact to Mawlana.

- Nothing would change if the books included love in them. You cannot learn it via books. It cannot be defined through the lines in a book. Let me explain what love is. You should burn the books first. Do not seek love in lovers. Love is not the mirror of the lover, so mirror is not sold in the bazaar of the blind. Love is not a word that you may write in a notebook. It destroys the paragraphs. This is why it cannot fit in the books. Books are for interpretations. Love itself is an endless path. One who enters in this path does not have any right to return. Do not complain about the holes and mud on the way. It is love that makes mud. Do not forget that you were created out of the meeting of light, which is called "the soul" with the body that is called "mud"...

I have the habit of praying with Jewish people and say "May Allah lead them to the right way". I even pray for those who swear at me and say "May Allah give them better ways than swearing" so that they may remember Allah and direct themselves towards the spiritual realism.

I told myself "what good is eating and drinking for unless I speak to Allah directly and get answers for my questions from Him? Did I come to this world merely for eating or drinking? I should ask him why I came here and where I will go; only then I may eat and sleep. Moreover, I should have enough information concerning my salvation and my end so that I may lead a comfortable and easy life here. This was my aim since my childhood and I sought it since then. Think of a mother that acts immediately and looks for cures to relieve her beautiful and charming child who has burnt his/her hand. Allah helps me in a similar way by His love.

I admire one who swears; but I am never fond of those who praise me. For, it would be worse to swear after that praise. The hypocrite is even worse than a disbeliever. It is said in the Quran, "The hypocrites will be in the lowest depths of the Fire" (4:145).

I have tamed my inner self to such a degree that; even if they put endless kebabs and desserts before me at a time when I am starving , I wouldn't look twice. Barley bread which is given to 'it' at an appropriate time is better than kebabs which are given inappropriately.

As it is known, even a lifeless being cannot endure me more than seven months. Those who listen to me at madrasas become mad, but why should I transform the intelligent ones into mad ones? Then I will not be able to talk with them. However, I cannot be and will not be a Sufi. That *dargah* is the place of pure ones. There is no trouble of cooking or shopping there. Even lifeless beings have a feeling of unity and separation (like atoms). The following verse of Quran is a sign for it, "There is not a thing but celebrates His praise; and yet ye understand not how they declare His glory! Verily He is oft- Forbear, most Forgiving! (17: 44)

MY QUEST

Oh Love, for whom I devoted my soul
Where art thou?

My youth was spent on searching for a spiritual master who would burn me in myself. I tried many shaykhs but realized that they cannot ignite a single spark even for themselves – not to speak of burning me. I knew that fame, properties and belongings might bring harm rather than profit and would aid me to devote myself to this lower world. The public was tired of continuous battles and despoils. They tended towards spiritual realm at least to find the inner peace, which they could not find here. I also had a great tendency towards Sufism. I hated those who said, "I am such and such person" in the *dargah*s. I was travelling from one country to another in the quest of a real spiritual master, a real shaykh.

This quest for a spiritual master whom would answer my questions satisfactorily, take me away from myself and whom I would devote myself to took years. No *dargah* (sufi gathering place) relieved me. I never lost my hope despite the existing emptiness inside me. Thus, I was at the age of sixty and my black beard turned to be white. I had a haircloth cardigan on my back, an *alâm* (staff) in my hand, and a hat (in fact a fur cap) on my head. I sometimes worked, carried things on my back and earned a few coins to make my living. I never demanded anything from people and I was never dependent on anyone. I was mostly hungry and making fun of my *self* (*nafs*). My *self* suffered a lot. I sometimes slept on a branch of a tree or on a rock. Yet – mostly- I used to sleep in a coffin and go to the mosque when I heard the call for Morning Prayer.

As I was thinking over the message 'what you sought is in Konya', two memories came to my mind. Firstly, I saw a crowded caravan which moved from Balh and passed by Damascus for pilgrimage. This unusual group attracted my attention. Mawlana was a five-year-old child and I was a teenager. I listened to his father, Baha al-Din, preaching on Friday in the mosque. I enjoyed his intellectual eloquence. I think my familiarity with Mawlana sparkled because of his father.

The other event occurred as I was walking at the bazaar in Damascus. I saw a man, who was at the age of forty; he was walking with some people. I could not stop looking at him and approached him suddenly. I held his arm and said:

- Oh the jeweler of the world, find me.

Then I left him. He was from Konya. It was he who carried what I looked for in him.

I made up my mind. I had to go to Konya and find this famous man. I took my staff and set off. People were talking about him wherever I went. They were telling each other how great his father was and even the non-Muslims admired him. A voice from inside whispered to me, "Go and see if he is honey or poison." I used to recite the following prayer as I lay in bed after my prayers:

- Oh Lord, let me meet friends. I prayed using the same supplication as I was lying on harvested crops in Aleppo. Then I fell asleep. I was told in my dream that this wish would be fulfilled but I should go to Anatolia. Then I was asked what I could give in return for this gift. I said:

- My head. I set off as soon as I woke up. I heard his name and fame as I was travelling in Anatolia. I decided to go to Konya. If I could find him, I would be saved. With this intention, I started my journey.

I saw a man in Urfa. He was not wailing although he was whipped. The more he was whipped the quieter he became. I followed him and asked why he was whipped. He said he was exposed to this punishment because he loved a lady. I asked, "Why did not you weep despite the pain?"

He said, "My beloved was looking at me". Then I said: "What if you knew the Almighty sees you all the time!" he fell down suddenly. I experienced a spiritual intuition in Prophet Abraham's *hajlagah* (tomb; lit. the bride room. Among *mawlawis,* cemeteries are called *hamushan*, ie.the silent ones.)

"Oh lord who shielded Ibrahim from the flames when he was thrown into the fire by Nimrod! My heart is full of such flames and these flames are so grand that I need you to help me find that friend that will put out this fire within me. Let the breath of lovers be wind beneath my wings that I may fly to Konya as soon as possible "I prayed. I was *paranda* that is the flying one. If the eyes of the one in the air are looking for dead bodies on the ground, what is flying for? Look, vultures also fly casting their black shadows. Is there anyone who can fly beyond the heart?

I was in Diyarbakir a week later. I lost my way from morning until noon prayer. After three days of walking, I climbed to the peak of a mountain. I could see a steep slope, a river and a village beyond that slope. As the village was far away, it seemed as small as a ring and the hills were as small as children were. In short, I submitted my heart to death and began rolling downwards. Those villagers who saw me thought that I was a monster, tiger or a creature as such. I was rolling as if sliding on my paws from the steep slope. When I arrived at the village, they came and prostrated in front of me. Looking at me in astonishment, they said, "How is it that he fell down yet has no injuries? May it be that he is *Khidr* or perhaps a genie?"

I left Diyarbakir immediately. It was night and felt like I was walking in my dream. I was in a sweet hurry to arrive at Konya as soon as possible. It was as if I was looking for Mawlana for years and he was waiting for me. I was full of intentions of openings. I was rushing towards Konya as if my homeland and my lips were dry from the thirst of the unknown one, which was Mawlana.

I am approaching you. My breath is as burning as the desert wind and is as freezing as the desert night..

A group of Sufis accompanied me while I was going to Erzincan. They assigned me as their leader and said: "We will not go anywhere without your approval. Even if we offend each other we won't do anything without your permission." They found no food to eat for a few days. It was the season of melons. One of the owners of a vegetable patch shouted out at us: "Oh Dervishes! Come and say bismillah ' in the name of God' and eat." They attempted to go there." "We are hungry. If you are hungry too, it is no use rejecting this miracle." Then I said, "That garden will remain there forever. Do you remember the account of a *Sufi* in which he carried a piece of bread in his pocket; "if I find something better than you, I would eat it. If not, you are in my pocket and I will eat you." We covered our ears and pretended to be deaf. We asked what the matter was with our gestures. He came nearer and insisted. I said, "Only by the condition that he would give the dervishes some of the melons that he was eating." He bowed down in reverence. In fact, he intended to give melons to dervishes. I said, "Eat ye the best ones and give the bad ones for God's sake. "The man mourned and fell down in agony. He hosted them for three more days. He sacrificed a few sheep. I said, "That's enough. You hosted these dervishes for seven days and you should now take care of yourself. Then I set off for my journey again.

I arrived in Erzincan; I left my friends behind so nobody knew me. I had good times there. I played games and wrestled with people. Soon they realized who I was and said, "You are Shams indeed". I looked for a job for three days but no one hired me. They did not accept me since they thought I was weak. A rich man saw me as he was passing by. He sent his servant to learn what I was looking for. I said, "Are you the keeper of this path? Tell me if are governing the city and the way." In short, he brought some delicious food and knelt down before me. After enjoying the meal he said, "Come and enjoy this food as long as you stay in this city." This sentence prevented me to leave the city.

One day, he saw me and said, "Please help me with this problem, since a friendship cannot be one-sided: "There is a passage from one heart to another." My heart is burnt for your sake and why do you keep me veiled? What is the underlying reason for it? My principles are as follows: I treat ones whom I first like in a severe manner. Then I devote myself entirely to him. Goodness is such a thing that if you treat a five-year-old child in a good manner, that child would be just like your child. However, a brave man is one that knows what his master suffers from and how patient he is against these troubles. He even sees where they take his master. He feels what mysteries he attains and the thousands of troubles he faces without any fear.

I was to set off after praying *asr* (canonical prayer between noon and evening) in Sivas. I witnessed someone praying in one corner of the mosque:

- Lord, open me the gates of Mercy.

- Are the Lord's gates of Mercy closed that you want Him to open them? His gates of Mercy are wide open all the time. You'd better check whether your gates are open!

- How should I pray, then?

- Is there a better prayer other than abstaining from sins? You may not bring the world to the Hereafter… lead such a life that the world may bring you to the Hereafter.

I travelled in many cities. The dead bodies in the cities were more than those in graveyards. For me, anybody that was distant to love was dead. The dead ones spoke, as I remained silent.

I visited Sivas, Kayseri and Aksaray. I looked for an appropriate inn. I wanted to have a bath. I had to clean my coat. However, I could not find a good one. I decided to spend the night in a small mosque. I entered the mosque and fell asleep in a corner. The *muadhin* saw me after the *isha* prayer as he was locking the door and scolded me:

- Hey, who are you? Leave this place immediately and find somewhere else.

- Allow me to stay here tonight. I am a stranger. I have no place to sleep; I do not demand anything more. Allow me to sleep here.

The man became angrier. He began shouting and uttering some bad words. I felt disgraced and said:

- I hope your tongue swells at once. I left the mosque. In the meantime his tongue began swelling and blocked his throat. The Imam rushed to him due to his wheezing. He asked.

- What's going on here?

The *muadhin* pointed at me and said:

- It is he who caused this. Go and ask his forgiveness.

The imam came to me and said:

- Sir, that poor *muadhin* could not recognize you. Forgive him." he beseeched.

- All things to be said are said. This is God's decree. I cannot do anything. However, I may pray for him to die with faith and have no unease in the Hereafter.

I continued to walk. When the imam returned, the *muadhin* was already dead.

I approached Konya.

ARRIVAL TO THE LAND OF LOVE OF MAWLANA

If Allah takes anyone from your gate to the palace of love.
How can you say to that person "I do not love you" ?

Oh Konya, I have walked for years before coming to you. My life was spent on roads. I walked continuously. I had a coat as black as night and shoes, which were worn out; but I carried the sun in my eyes and the rivers that seek their beds inside me. I passed by roads that smelled like oleasters. The screams inside me were always before my steps. Where is my ocean, oh Konya!

My intentions concerning Konya were not aimless; for, my final hope was in Konya. I was told in my dreams that the spiritual master I sought was the sultan of Konya. The dreams and the roads pointed at him.

I arrived in Konya on a Thursday evening in November 1244. I was excited when I saw the Minarets of Konya from far away. I asked a boy where to find an inn to stay the night. He told me the way to Sekerciler Inn. The innkeeper looked at my face in a weird way and thought that I was a merchant.

- What is the very thing you came here to buy?
- I said:
- A diamond.
- Then, it is the wrong city. We have brass and silver works here. Moreover, our city is famous for gold work and weavers. You can also find lapis lazuli, pearls and onyx. However, we do not have diamonds here.

- You have a unique piece of diamond before you and you see nothing more than glass! Now, do not waste my time. Give me the keys to my room.

I went upstairs. There was a sofa covered with woolen cushions a carpet made of silk and a cotton mattress. I put all of them aside. The straw mat on the ground was enough for me. I broke my fast with a piece of bread and half a glass of water. I performed the night prayer. I washed my garments and hanged them on the wall. I said, "Let's see what Allah will show tomorrow" and fell asleep.

The following day was November the 25th. After praying the Morning Prayer, I recited some passages from the Holy Quran until the time of Friday prayer. Everybody around including women, men and children were staring at me. Their looks were bothering me as if to say I was the only stranger in the city or I had a different sign on me. I was sitting on the rocks in front of the inn and watching the passersby. I plunged into past reminiscences. My body remained in front of the inn, whereas my soul went back to the very moment of the first sight, to that talismanic sight in Damascus. I remembered the mysterious memory of the past. Once upon a time, both figures met in Damascus. Shams was addressing the public in front of the Great Mosque. Mawlana, who was having sleepless nights because of being caught by the clamp of doubt and distress, came closer to listen to the speaker. His voice was of another realm, a mysterious work. It was neither the words nor the meanings that shocked the listeners entirely; it was rather the tone, color and efficacy of the speech. However, Mawlana felt another taste; the words were burning him…

Mawlana fixed his gaze on Shams… his poverty, affliction and majesty… Shams also looked at him. At that very moment, their gazes united and there formed an infinite immortality inside them. Shams stopped speaking and disappeared.

Mawlana was looking for that person the owner of those burning words, as would a child whom just lost his mother would with hasty eyes. He was in agony, he could not find him. It was as if the ground split and swallowed Shams. As he was trying to understand what was happening in anxiety and curiosity, he startled suddenly by a hand on his shoulder. The source of his inner light said: "Oh the jeweler of the world, find me", then disappeared again like a vision. Seeing all these, Mawlana was in wonderment and felt an indefinable burning in his heart. He sat on the steps of Great Mosque to comfort his excitement. This event was forgotten soon afterwards. The wind blowing in his visions forced Mawlana to leave Damascus. Therefore, he returned to Konya.

Today the sun in Damascus rose in Konya. The great ocean dragged along a single drop. Now that Mawlana did not dive into the ocean although he came by the shore, Shams carried mountains on his back and deserts in his hands so that the ocean may attain the drop.

I woke up from my dream when I heard "He is coming…" It was almost afternoon. There was a flutter and bewilderment in the streets of the bazaar. I thought that an emperor was approaching as I saw the preparations and the joy of people around. People in the street moved towards both sides and the ones in the shops went out. Those who were sitting there stood up and joined their hands on their bellies. I said "what a ceremony, what a fussiness of respect." However, the one who was approaching was obviously a scholar. He was coming accompanied by his students. Everyone said:

- Mawlana Jalal al-Din is coming.

They were standing and greeting him. I thought that this was Mawlana whom I have heard about for years and saw once in Damascus; He should be the one on the mule with a black beard, dark skin and a smile. I liked his attitude and spiritual state. I thought that this is the diamond for the sake of which I came here. I stood up and followed the crowd that gradually became more and more as they saw the crowd moving into the narrow streets. It was necessary to listen to the advice of this renowned spiritual guide.

All though he was in front of the crowd the back of his turban was visible. It was as if a beam of light was emanating from his turban. I knew that if I called out to him he would turn back and fall down in to my arms from the mule, but I was able to control myself. I was aware of the fact that the friends should meet in the hall of love before beginning to walk towards the palace of unity hand in hand.

I rushed towards him among the crowd. Mawlana was lost in contemplation and was not aware of the people around. I took the bridle from the old man's hand and stopped the mule. The old man resisted, but my dissolving sight sufficed to silence him.

- Are you Mawlana, son of the Sultan of scholars, Baba Walad? Mawlana said in surprise as his eyes were wide open:
- Yes, it is me.
- Tell me who is greater- saint Bûyezid of Bistam or Prophet Mohammed?

Mawlana spurred his mule:

- What kind of question it is? Of course, Prophet Mohammed is greater.

I allowed the old man to take the bridle and the crowd continued to walk. On the other hand, I had not finished my words. I shouted after him:

- If Prophet Mohammed is greater, then why did he say "Oh Lord, I could not know you as you deserve" and Bayezid said "I praise myself! How exalted I am. For, I am full of Truth."

The mule stopped and Mawlana turned back on the saddle. He tried to remember this man. Did they meet before? Mawlana's first reply was spontaneous, but he was careful this time:

- Prophet Mohammed was still looking for Allah and none he knew sufficed to stop searching. However, Bayezid was lost in Allah. He thought he attained Allah, but there was no attainment as such.

He turned around on the mule and they disappeared among the people. I murmured, "Good answer". Yes, I was right; this was the man I was looking for. I did not pass all those roads in vain. I went on following him. I wished Mawlana would turn and look at me. I wished for him to only look once and burn immediately. I went on following him in excitement so that he may turn back. The people around were curious about what was happening there. I did not care about the public. Whom I cared was the one who was riding the mule.

The crowd arrived at Karatay Madrasa and I stopped at a corner nearby the tiled dome. Everybody was sitting whereas I was standing and staring at him. "How serious he is in his garments!"

The madrasa was vibrating in expectation. The roar of hoarse voices was reflecting on the walls. The blue sky was penetrating inside from the lamp in the middle of the dome. There was a pond just under the dome as a mirror used by the astrologist for observing the stars at night. One of his students put some books on a table before Mawlana and everybody sat around it. As he was preparing for his speech, I said – thinking that this was an opportunity:

- To have knowledge and to know are completely different concepts. Knowledge is only a part of memory. In this respect, you can be a gnostic. To go beyond knowing is the journey of our soul beyond visible realm in which case you can be a lover. Now tell me Mawlana, who are you?

He raised his head and looked at me in such a way that I fainted immediately. When I gained my conscious, he was waiting next to my bed. He took my hands and brought me to his madrasa. We entered a cell. This cell belonged to a jeweler, Salah al-Din. We stayed there for a while.

Mawlana said,

- Oh my Sultan! I know you visited many cities. Why did you have the trouble of coming here instead of practicing spiritual guidance there? I smiled and said:

- I always met incapable pharaohs there; I met people who were not content with being a slave of God. You are the only real servant I have ever met.

- Oh Shams al-Din Tabrizi, oh the pearl of spiritual realm! I know my house is not one you deserve but I am a loyal servant. What belongs to a servant is the property of his master. This is your house now and then; my children are your sons and daughters.

He gave all his belongings under my service and won my heart.

I also wanted to put him on trial. I wondered whether he would choose the simple way as the previous masters did or endure all difficulties in order to gain the secret. Mawlana was a distinguished person that I could not conceive. He was not a regular *hodja*; however, he was in such a state that he was abstaining from indicating his hunger behind the veils of those around him. It was as if we were two wrestlers who wished to measure each other's strength on a platform. I was looking for a shaykh and he was in search of one. We were like two falcons waiting to quench their thirst nearby a fountain. I wanted him to bring me some wine, as I demanded from *Awhad al-Din Kermani* once. Mawlana submitted himself before my wish against the sights of wonderment and amazement of other people. He rushed to a Greek inn and brought the wine himself. I poured the wine, as he was looking at me in surprise.

I never drink wine. I wanted it, because I wished to test your loyalty. I wanted to understand whether you were like the others or not. You have a superior station than I imagined. You have passed the initial trials one by one. Let us see what you will do next. No one can be equal to you as you have such a strength and endurance.

Mawlana embraced me in joy. He embraced me in such a joy that it was as if he attained a bliss, which everyone was eager to gain. At that very moment, I got rid of the weariness of years and the burdens as big as mountains. I praised Allah for bestowing me with such a friend after many years. I stood up and prayed two *rakah*s in gratitude. His small madrasa, which was used as house, was surrounded by mystery and became full of love and spirituality.

He was a *mudarris* who taught his students, an admired admonisher preaching in mosques, a public *mufti* who was trying to solve the problems of people via his *fatwa*s until that very day. Now he is away from everyone and everything, sitting cross-legged in a circle of love for my spiritual conversation. He said,

- Unless I find a sign from you I would not be able to attain a sign of soberness even if I went to the East, the West or. I used to be a renowned ascetic; I had a pulpit and high rank. Now my heart has transformed me into a lover who admires you.

You have this or that, you have "that person said this" and "told that"
However, what do you have inwardly of thyself, Mawlana?

One day I sat by the fountain in the madrasa and began invoking. Mawlana came with some books. I knew that he never gave up reading from the time I arrived there. I thought, "Oh poor one, he thinks that he would find what he looks for in those pieces of paper. What have you gained after all those years of reading?" He smiled and sat down next to me.

- Have you read many of those books?
- Yes, I read day and night.
- What have you gained then? Give them to me; let me see. Is this the one your father wrote?
- Yes, it is my father's own work.
- And that scrap is the poetry of that lunatic so-called *Mutanabbi*?
- Indeed.
- All right then. Give me all those useless volumes one by one.

He gave them to me. I began throwing them into the pond one by one. In the meantime, his disciples could not understand what was going on. They were surprised. Mawlana saw that all those books, which he spent many years reading, were thrown into the pond and turned the pond into a sea of ink. He began crying. The disciples jumped into the pond immediately trying to save the books. I raised my voice and shouted:

- Stop there. This is none of your business. Leave us alone.

Mawlana knelt down. He was crying while looking at his favorite masterpieces. He seemed sorrowful. I smiled and looked at him. I entered the pond and collected the books one by one.

- Is this the one you wanted?

I gave it to Mawlana.

- Amazingly *Asrarname* still had dust on it. It was as if taken from the library shelves rather than the water.

The science of love cannot be learnt in madrasa. In addition, books cannot inform us of love. If you have the intention to learn love, have you learnt anything at school? I do not want to see books in your hands. I do not allow you to read even your father's *Maarif*. You have this and that but what hath thou of yourself? Until which moment will you quench your thirst under the shadow of your father or other people? If I had not done so that very day, Mawlana would neither have understood love nor would the people be gifted with those great works including his "*Mathnawi*" which stemmed from his longing for me after my parting.

FROM SPIRITUAL RETREAT (HALWAH) TO NOCTURNAL JOURNEY (MIRAJ)

Mohammad emerged out of love,
What emerges out of love without Mohammad?

H*alwah* means to stay alone and seclusion in a corner in Arabic. In Sufism, it means to be placed by a spiritual master into a dark place isolated from the outer world in order to practice contemplation and to realize mortification of the flesh via some special invocations. It can be defined as communicating with God secretly; and purifying and saving the heart from misbelief and evil deeds. From this respect, it expresses to submit the entire being to Allah Himself and leaving all other than Him aside.

Halwah emerged from the Prophet's seclusion practice before the Revelation in the cave *Hira*. By the inspiration of Prophet Moses on Mount Tur for forty days, *halwat* was intended to last for forty days. Halwat was also called *arbain* (lit. forty days in Arabic) or *chila*. However, the main aim of *halwah* is keeping the mind and thought away from everything other than Allah.

Some think that we are speaking about some mysterious and veiled things behind closed doors. How curious they are. Nevertheless, our *halwah* or counsel is obvious for spiritual people. What is *dargah* for troubles is known (*agah*) for us.

They think that we spend our entire day in laziness. They think that *halwah* is losing oneself in between four walls. To lead a simple life is quite absurd for lovers. The saints are regarded as lunatic at first glance by those who fear love itself. The saint does not care about being regarded as mad or crazy. They do not pay attention to smaller facts. However, they would not have the slightest indication about the profound troubles and dark whirlpools we have have passed.

Halwah is Mawlana's lectern. If it wasn't for our *halwah*, gaining maturity would take longer or even be impossible.

He may begin his day by the interpretation of the Quran. We were walking along the passage of Sufism. Each *halwah* was a journey towards a station by covering the stones on the walls via Horasan mortar. A station in which the seeker is molded by *Ilm al-Yakin* (the knowledge of certainty), *Ayn al-Yakin* and *Haqqa'l Yakin*. As the outer voices and the intervention of social life would separate one from the spiritual realm, I secured Mawlana for outer facts. It is possible to reach the inward state only by being deaf to outward or being closed for outer facts. This was possible only by *halwah*.

We were constantly praying. Some unseen beings accompanied us during the fast of attainment (*wisal*) and the prayers of divinely awe. The people in the dargah thought that only Shams and Mawlana were in the room. They could not see those beings with us. And they would not be able to see them.

Our seclusion was being spent by question and answers; and sometimes as conversations in which I spoke and Mawlana listened or Mawlana spoke and I listened.

We were talking on everything concerning the universe. We were internalizing everything on love. My severe questions were compelling Mawlana. I did not want any stove, heater or fire in our room. My tongue sufficed to be fire. I have never liked the heat. There is nothing better than perspiring in coldness!

In our counsels, there were times when Mawlana was trembling and fainted.

They asked Mansur, "What does love stand for?" He said be patient. You will see it within three days. They cut his arms and feet off. Each organ bespoke love. They hanged his body and it proclaimed love. They burnt and poured his ashes into the river. Each atom said Ana'l Ishq (it is I who am love) in reverence."

In the early days of *halwah*, we were staying in our cell. When I told him that we would perform the fast of attainment (*wisal*), he was surprised. He could not say anything. He probably thought that it was impossible to practice such a fast that was not lawful according to Islamic rules. In order to remove his doubt, I told him that this sort of fasting was lawful for "prophets and lovers".

- If you intend to be a lover, you should begin with the fast of attainment. Your attainment is to remove the veil of attaining. I think you are anxious about it. Let me explain what the fast of attainment is: to fast three or four days continuously without breaking (*iftar*) it:

We shared the same state after the days of spiritual seclusion but I had to test him to see if he was ready for my secrets. These trials were of importance. I would leave Konya secretly if he would hesitate even in a slightest manner.

He knocked my door one morning.

- Come, my dear Mawlana! Sit down. Would you do me a favor if I wished?
- Of course, I will.

- Bring me a woman to entertain me. He stood up. He brought his wife Kira Hatun soon.
- She is my sister in both worlds. I do not want her.

Why did you bring her instead of bringing another one from the street? Are not you possesive of her? Or do you have any idea concerning my intention?

Mawlana allowed her to go out. Then he said, "You are away from lust and women. Thus, I understood that you were testing me and I brought Kira. At the same time, my message in doing so was that all I have was devoted in your way.

What if I wanted some wine? – would you go to the shop of that Jew and bring it yourself or order a disciple of yours to bring it?

- I would go and bring it myself.
- Good. It is you whom I sought for years. I was right. Now I can teach you meanings that you desire to fill the emptiness inside you. I will be your teacher and you will be mine. Do not forget… you are ready for my severe troublesome or sometimes testing attitudes in order to transform your old ruined state into a magnificent one. I said we would be united from moment to moment within such state of sharing. He nodded and raised his hand on to the left side of his chest (which means I am ready for your service). Then he left my room.

I found what I sought when I was young in old age
Either I came early or you are late for attainment… it is destiny!

My soul became acquainted with Mawlana whose destiny was determined on path by this resemblance first. His life was in accordance with migration. Both travelers, both seekers would meet on the predestined day. I found him and he found me on the same path. People call our second meeting as "*Maraja'l Bahrayn*" (the meeting of two oceans-t.n.). We did not overflow.

I traveled so much and used many fragrances. However, I had not found anyone who knew as much as he did. My heart was not contented with whatever *dargah* I visited. The scholars were alike. All were disciples before me and all were pebbles in my eyes. I found the diamond in Konya. I used to listen to those so-called spiritual masters who claimed that they were masters. Then I used to ask them whether their speech was over. When they said yes, I would tell them that I had a question for them. They would begin huffing, puffing, and perspiring. Those who were accompanying them would also groan. They would even lynch me if allowed. I would leave their circles when they lost their sense of patience. The ones whom I would test as spiritual masters became my disciples. I never wanted masses; I had nothing to do with disciples. I needed spiritual masters. Then I used to set off for another place. The inns were my houses. I would stay in various inns. If I went to a small town or a village, I would climb on a tree and sleep there.

I liked nights. Therefore, my only garment was a black coat in my whole life. Once Mawlana put a big chest of cloth given to him before me.

I said,

- What are these?
- Indian cloth
- Where did they come from?
- They are presents from the Sultan.
- …
- Let us make a robe for you, Shams.

I laughed and said, "Cloth will became nails and they would torture my body. Give them to the poor. My black coat is enough for me. I have carried it on my back for years.

- Why is it black?
- I like "nights"! The strangers are people of darkness. I will die in a certain night. He was silent.

I would never talk to those who wanted to be my friends unless putting them on trial. Test your friend. In that case, it would be certain whether they are friends or not. The coward ones cannot be friends.

Let us understand love first.
Why is not there any love in the qibla of those who say love is the beginning of everything?
Let us start from love. My dear Mawlana, Let us see what is at the end of the way?

We sat down on a cushion cross-legged and began counseling. Jalal al-Din was almost at the right state I wished from the very day I came there. When I spoke, he would listen so carefully that sometimes I did not enjoy speaking and did not like the way he listened. Then I would change the course of our conversations into question and answer.

- Do you know, my dear Mawlana, Allah never bestows love over idle ones. For He wants love to belong only to Himself. Love is in Him and emerges from Him. As a matter of fact, the love for Allah is one which is firm and unsurpassable. This love means to remember Allah by heart and tongue continuously, to establish a firm friendship with Him, abstain from everything that separates us from Him, and to contemplate over His Bliss and Bounties. Thus, one knows Allah as He inspired Himself via generosity, mercy and beneficence.
- Then, what comes first – love or obedience?
- The beginning of love is obedience. However, obedience is other than Divine love; for love begins with obedience. In fact, Allah informs his Majesty to people and leads them to obey Him. Then make them love – without being in need of them. He makes love peculiar to Himself and places it to his lovers' hearts. Due to the intenseness of

luminosity of love in their hearts, Allah let them wear the apparent light in their words. When Allah leads them to the existing state, He gives them to the angels due to the contentment for them.

Allah created the universe out of love; thus love forms the majority of existents in the universe. Allah never ceases to love creatures; He never stops creating them. Everything is intertwined with love and mixed with it; for the Divine Attribute "Love" brings them into existence and it moves all their acts and actions.

We may understand the following saying of the Prophet "Allah is beautiful and He likes Beauty" in the following way: He defined Himself as He loves Beauty; so He loves the universe. He is beautiful; when beauty becomes something essentially loved, the whole universe loves Allah. The love of a part of the universe towards another part is a reflection of Allah's love for Himself.

"There is no lover and beloved except for Allah."

To seek the Friend became obligatory for Lovers
Like the floods crawling into His River.

In fact, He is the seeker and we are like shadows,
It is He who speaks in all our speeches.

Either we flow in friend's river like floods
Or are imprisoned in His goblet as water.

We say "Oh friend, our friend" although we are with the Friend,
We say, "Where art thou?" next to Him out of intoxication.

Love is also as such. No one loves other than The Creator; however, all love towards *Zaynab, Suad, Hind, Hurshid* or world, money, rank and everything loved that are veiled from Him because of love. The poets spend their words and images on these elements; but they are unaware of them. The sages never hear a verse, a dilemma, poem or ode, which is not concerning Allah who is behind the veil of forms. All the hopes, desires and passions of people towards various things – such as mother, father, friends, heavens, earth, gardens, palaces, knowledge, food and drinks, etc. – are desires for Allah and all of them are veils. When people see the Eternal Sultan without these veils, they will understand that all these are but veils and the object of all desires is in fact that "only Being". All their difficulties will be resolved, all questions in their hearts will be answered and they will see everything clearly.

Each love is in fact love for Allah. Love is good; for, it is divine; however, if lovers define its true object, it will remain as an illusory veil.

Love is an attribute of Allah who is in need of nothing
The love for any other thing is only a metaphor.

It is golden plated, for, the beauty of others
Seems brilliant but their inward consisted of darkness.

When the gleams disappear and smoke becomes apparent
The metaphorical love becomes frozen then.

Beauty returns to its source,
What remains from me is only that is coarse and corrupted.

As the moonlight returns to the moon,
Its reflection vanishes on the wall.

- What do lovers fear and what do they hope for, oh Shams?
- They fear losing what the hearts gained in the past. Then they are anxious due to the fear that never leaves the

heart of all lovers. They fear for being ungrateful to the bounties The Beloved bestowed unto them and to be deprived of these bounties as a result. Thus, when fear is placed in their hearts and the self begins plunged into hopelessness, their hopes gain strength as they remember the broadness of Allah's Mercy. The hope of Lovers is to attain the truth and to approach it via some means. In this way – as they are between fear (*hawf*) and hope (*raja*) – they never become distant from His service and obedience towards Him; and they act in all their deeds in accordance with His Decree. For, they know that He promised to tolerate them. Did not you hear about this verse: "Gracious is Allah to His servants: He gives Sustenance to whom He pleases: and He has power and can carry out His Will" (Quran, 42:19).

All sustenance means Grace. The Grace in Allah's loving especially him apart from all creatures is obvious. In fact, when love is situated in a servant's heart, to remember neither human beings and genies nor Paradise or hell and anything other than the beloved is virtuous for him. The beloved finds virtue and pleasure only in remembering vices those that departed him from his beloved, his Power and Generosity just as the Allah's deliverance of his Messenger Ibrahim Khalil from the great fire set for him. Thus, Allah, the Owner of Majesty and Beauty showed Ibrahim Khalil the signs of His Power and his aid to the ones who sought Him without any recompense. This is what the lovers remember the following promises given by Allah to his saintly servants: They will attain Allah (in this world) and their veils will be removed; they will not grieve on the Resurrection Day when everyone would be subject to deadly fears of that fearful day.

- What is passion for you?
- For me, it is a candle which takes radiance from the light of love and which is not an excess over the essential love.
- What is real love?

- It is love of faith. The Almighty witnesses the love the believers have for Him and says, "But those people of faith are overflowing in their love for Allah" (Quran, 2:165).

Now, the luminosity of passion is of the light of love. The excess of love emerges from the love of friendship. The passion takes an action only by the light of friendship in the heart. Thus, when Allah lights the candle of passion in a servant's heart, it is not passion that takes action in the plains of the heart, but the heart illuminates by it. Only looking at it from the eye of faith may extinguish this candle. When the servant is sure about the enemies in his deeds, he moves away from the anxiety of abondoning his deeds.

Mawlana lowered his head in silence. He began thinking and the room was filled by a deep silence. He raised his right hand on to his chest and asked,

- Will there be a chance for us to see the Supreme Beloved?
- Know it well that the vision of saints is not like seeing people, matters, species, substances, contingencies, attributes and names on a spatial plane. To see God is a notion that is honorable and superior to all these and it is above all attributes and qualities. This sight is the sight of a light in light and for light. Thus, Allah says, "Allah is the Light of the heavens and the earth. The Parable of His Light is as if there was a Niche and within it a Lamp: the Lamp enclosed in Glass: the glass as it were a brilliant star: lit from a blessed Tree, an Olive, neither of the east nor of the west, whose oil is well-nigh luminous, though fire scarce touched it: Light upon Light! Allah doth guide whom He will to His Light: Allah doth set forth Parables for men: and Allah doth know all things." (Quran, 24:35)
- After hearing my words, Mawlana shouted aloud the Supreme Name, "Allaaah". Then began whirling (*sama*) after pronouncing the following verses:

No one is in such a worse state than the lover on the earth,
When he finds the pleasure of passion
You see that the lover cries all the time,
Either out of desire or of the fear for separation…
When he attains the beloved, he cries out of the fear for separation
And when he is away from the beloved, out of enthusiasm.
Yes, the eyes of lover burst into tears
Either in separation or attainment for the Beloved.

As he fell down after *sama*, I wanted him to regain his strength and said:

- Allah is the first Beloved and all existents desire Him, turn to Him and all the works will be inclined to Him. Because the existence, intensity, the continuity and perfection of all existents is only by Him. He is the only One whose existence is by Himself. Oh brother, may Allah let you attain His Essence and perfect your light as He promised for his elect servants and saints. The mentioned good news is from the following verse of Quran:

"Their Light will run forward before them and by their right hands, while they say, "Our Lord! Perfect our Light for us, and grant us Forgiveness: for Thou hast power over all things." (Quran, 66:8)

Mawlana shot ahead suddenly. He embraced me so strongly that it was as if all my bones were broken. He was kissing my cheeks and caressing my beard.

- May Allah lead you and all our true brothers to the right way. May He lead you and us to the truth. In fact, He bestows His Mercy on His servants.

- Human beings are of three groups, Jalal al-Din. Firstly, they were beaten by the stick of affliction and killed by the sword of eagerness. They wait for beneficence before the Divine gate. Secondly, they were beaten by the stick of repentance and killed by the sword of penitence. They wait for the forgiveness before the Divine gate. Thirdly, they were beaten by the stick of forgetfulness and killed by the sword of lust. They wait for punishment before His Gate."

Know it well that love has three essential levels: human love, spiritual Love and Divine love. Human love is the initial phase of love and a step to spiritual love. The spiritual love is the ladder for Divine love. Divine love is apparent only to those whose substance is pure, matter is gentle, appearance is elegant, nature is refined, soul is kind, secret is luminosity and creation is supreme. Thus, love can be found in those who possess beauty, perfection and morality. For, the nature of love drags the ores of beauty as magnet.

Love is adorned by the Beauty of God who created everything out of His Beauty. One attains spiritual love gradually when he falls in love from the point of the condition of eternal beauty trusted to Adam. Spiritual love was illuminated by the sparkles of souls in the mines of eternal beauty. God manifested Himself on those souls with all His attributes and his Beauty as He created them. When man reaches perfection within these two levels and attains the teaching of both loves, he conforms to Allah's love for him in eternity. This condition is stated in the following verse: "Allah loves them and they love Him."

The Holy Prophet (P.B.U.H) says,

"Allah says, 'When my servant is busy mostly with me, I transform his lust into seeking and inclining towards Me. In doing so, my servant loves Me and I love Him. When he forgets Me, I immediately intervene between him and forgetfulness. These are my real saints and they are truly brave ones. When I will bring down a calamity, I cancel it for their sake."

His love consists of the manifestation of Divine Love in him by the manifestation of Divine Beauty (*Jamal*). For this reason, it is said, "Prophet David fell in love with Allah". Likewise, Arabs said, "Muhammad fell in love with his Lord."

Everybody else drinks wine and becomes intoxicated,
We are people of love; we became drunk even without drinking.

It was springtime in Konya. We took a stroll towards Meram Gardens, which Mawlana liked very much. I offered to get there on foot. He did not refuse my offer. We set off without taking any food and drink from the *dargah* or bazaar. When we arrived at Meram, we sat down under an oak tree by the river. The nightingales were singing so efficiently that the sound of the water and the songs of nightingales were ascending our souls over the clouds. A few Greek people were cooking meat and drinking wine under a tree a few meters away. Mawlana was looking at them. Then he turned to me and said:

- Oh Shams, may I ask a question?
- Of course.
- Why do you test people with wine? You also wanted me to bring a bottle of wine once.
- The secret is in ripen ones and love flows in their veins. To find the real ripen people, you should test them with the sin which they fear most. In this case, it is wine that they abstain for the fear that people would criticize oneself; one can lose his prestige and his superior position among the society. Those whom I met before you lost this burdensome trial even before beginning. You also have not passed this trial of wine. You only succeeded in the first phase. Remember that one day you will have another trial. I am not quite sure that you will succeed in it. When I feel you are

ready, your trial will begin immediately. Now can you see any distinction between us and the drunken ones sitting over there?

- Do you mean that we are also drunk?

- Being drunk is pleasure in which one understands the words and "the intellect" that discerns the power to make distinction. Allah says, "O ye who believe! Approach not prayers with a mind befogged, until ye can understand all that ye say" (Quran, 4:43). Here Allah lays down a condition that one should understand what is said to him in order not to be regarded as intoxicated. When he begins to understand what is said, he is the out of the drunkenness state according to the majority of scholars. You like jurists. Now tell me how your scholars define it?

- When they asked *Imam Ahmed bin Hanbal*, "How is it possible to know that one is drunk?", he said, "If he cannot discern his garments from those of anyone else and his shoes from those of anybody else…" It is narrated from *Imam Shafii* (May Allah bestow him His Mercy): "If one's regular words become nonsense and if he reveals his secret, he is considered as drunk."

Dawud al-Isfahani said, "If one's grieves are dispersed and unveils the secrets, he is considered as drunk".

- Drunkenness comprises two meanings: the existence of taste and deprivation of the ability to discern. When drunkenness is mentioned, either one of them or both of them are referred. There are certainly some passions and lusts that the self will enjoy when it comes across them. Nevertheless, to know there exists ugliness whether they occur now or at a certain moment later helps one restrain himself from such pleasures. The intellect orders the self not to commit it. However, when the intellect that enjoins (goodness) and the knowledge that manifests (the vices) disappear, the self plunges into its passions and becomes ready to commit everything.

The reason for drunkenness may be this test or sometimes the grief itself. Allah says, "O mankind! fear your Lord! for the convulsion of the Hour (of Judgment) will be a thing terrible! The Day ye shall see it, every mother giving suck shall forget her suckling- babe, and every pregnant female shall drop her load (unformed): thou shalt see mankind as in a drunken riot, yet not drunk: but dreadful will be the Chastisement of Allah." (Quran, 22:1-2)

Another reason for intoxication is the joy a lover feels when he sees the beloved. In this case, his words become meaningless and his acts change as he loses his intellect. This joy can even kill him by a natural course: the blood in the heart spreads more than usual (the circulation of blood speeds up) and the blood that transmits the required heat falls. The heart cools down and causes death. Now you have understood how lovers become drunk. If you go and bring some wine from those man, the wine won't be able to make us drunk instead it, itself will become drunken. Let us enjoy Meram now.

I will tell you words those that are without tongues and lips
I will tell something concealed from the ears
I will speak among everyone but none will hear my words except you.

Mawlana gradually reached the state I wished for him in our seclusions; however, his ears were not closed for the outside. It had been a while since he stopped reading books. I changed his life; there was no trace of his past life, but I had to be sure that he had no residues in his heart.

- Mawlana, I cannot give you the secrets without purification of your water, know it well that no ablution can be performed with muddy water. "…soon will Allah produce a people whom He will love as they will love Him" (Quran, 5:54)
- Are you ready to enter the path of love? Do you think that you gained such perfectness? Oh my dear Mawlana, you are not fully ripen yet.
- Aren't I fully ripen yet? What should I do to be ripen and unveil that veil of mysteries?
- What is the "self", Mawlana?
- The self is to be yourself. Prophet Isa (Jesus) said: "Thou knowest what is in my heart, Thou I know not what is in Thine. For Thou knowest in full all that is hidden." (Quran, 5:116).

Shams said:

- To forge, to recite Yasin into ears of a donkey.

- Few people contemplate and search on their own "self". It is your physical body that you see in a mirror but you see your self in your heart.

Your words are so valuable Mohammed. You said mirror:

"To Allah belong the East and the West: whithersoever ye turn, there is Allah's face. For Allah is All-Embracing, All-Knowing." (2:115)

- If He had not looked at us, we would cease to exist. The sages climb from the skirts of metaphors to the summit of truth and perfect their ascension.

- Oh Shams! I am cooked and melted. Lead me to the mystery of mysteries. Will you invite me to the mysterious treasure of love?

- Do you think that you are cooked (ripen)?
- Praise be to the Lord.
- Are you serious?
- Glorious is Allah.
- Are you sincere in this?
- I have faith in it.
- Then you are ready for your last trial.
- If He wills.
- You will go to Sille on foot tomorrow morning. You will get a big jug of wine from the Greek inn and bring it to the *dargah* during the day. Will you do it?
- For sure.
- But people would condemn you.
- I do not care.
- And scholars will announce negative *fatwa*s against you.
- I would not care less.
- They will gossip about you in Konya.
- Damn them.
- All right then. Let us wait until tomorrow and see if you are sincere or not.

The following morning, Mawlana set off alone without informing anyone. He got a jug of wine. He was coming to *dargah* wearily. The wine jug or pot was different from other ones by its form and color. It was sunny and almost everybody was in the streets. Mawlana was walking as he had the jug on his back. The streets, roads and the bazaar were full of people. Those who saw him could not believe their eyes. The man who preached and taught them for years and whom they praised as a scholar was carrying a wine jug on his back. It cannot be true. They were thinking silently but then they began pronouncing their complaints outwardly:

- Shame on you! What a strange Muslim he is. Did not he tell us in his sermons that drinking wine is unlawful and carrying it is also a sin.

The women were talking behind the windows.

- Woe to him! Look what he is doing now. The shopkeepers said:
- God's wrath is near. If a *hodja* carries wine, it means that the Doomsday is near.

Mawlana was approaching his *dargah* in weariness without paying attention to what was being said. I and a few other dervishes were waiting for him at the front gate. He came along with a group of curious people. His weariness was obvious from the sweat on his forehead. I told the dervishes to bring him water. I cleaned his forehead with my emerald handkerchief. He still had the wine jug on his back. People were wondering what the matter was. The crowd became greater including even some curious Christians and Jews. There was a huge stone by the door used at night to put behind the door for security. I jumped over it and took the wine jug from his back.

- Oh forgetful ones! oh idle ones who practice according to outward. You came here to reproach and blame him. You said, "How can a sage and scholar carry wine" and scolded him. You are obviously wrong. You are Muslim only outwardly. A cloak, rosary and beard are enough for you. You are deaf, blind and even ungrateful. Today, the entire Konya became losers and it is only Mawlana who won. You supposed that he carried wine. Take that wine and enjoy it! When he turned the jug upside down, it was only milk coming out of it.

Mawlana was surprised, too. He knelt down and began crying. I held his hands, and then I kissed him on the cheeks. I said:

- You passed the trial by the light of your soul.

We entered our cell. He sat on a cushion. I whispered in his right ear. He shouted, "Allah is the greatest" so powerfully that a baby sleeping in a house in another street would have woken up.

There is a secret hidden in the rhythm of music
The world would be upside down if I unveiled it.

We used to recite Holy Quran after every Morning Prayer together with Mawlana. I would recite and he would listen to it. One day he came and sat next to me after his invocations. I kissed the Quran and put it on the lectern.

- If Quran is a remembering (*dhikr*), then one's answer to it is also a remembering. It is a remembrance that Allah revealed by his messengers. Everything that reminds Allah is *dhikr*. There is no love without *dhikr*. The self cannot see itself in a mirror without love.

Some people invented a term called "the secret dhikr". Is there a closed remembrance? Is it possible to sell mirrors in the bazaar of the blind? Making noise is not invocation and staying still like a statue is not *rabita* (having the image of the spiritual masters during invocation-t.n.). *Dhikr* is *sama* and music. The invocation in the sound of the Nay (the reed flute) is more meaningful than the invocation of a thousand dervishes. We will play the Nay before the canonical prayers beginning tomorrow. Is it clear?

- All right, my dear Shams. Let us talk about music then.
- Sure. Speak and may meanings come to our soul out of your tunes.
- Music is also remembering of Allah. The flowing of water and leaves of trees are also remembrance of Him. The universe came into existence by music.

- Music is the reflection of our voice in the creation of our souls. The sounds convey our love to Allah and it is the caressing of our soul.
- There was no *sama* before you and music as well. There was no love either. Shams came and Mawlana became a lover.

The words of Mawlana became like music and they caressed my soul. He had such a language of the state that literature would be helpless and eloquence would be afflicted before Mawlana's crystal river. I fell in love and fell in ecstasy. I proclaimed "Allaaah"; I called the dervish waiting outside the room:

- Bring me a piece of reed from my room! Mawlana was surprised. The reed had no holes on it. I blew at one end of the reed and there emerged an opening. Then I touched my fingers on it in an order. And the holes appeared. I said,
- We are like the nay and our tune comes from you. The first thing Allah created was reed and He blew His secret into it.

Mawlana said:

- Then may the nay in our *sama* be the horn of Raphael (*Israfil*). I nodded.

"Satan has all human features except for one. He does not know what love is. Satan was not given love. It was given to man. The jealousy of Satan emerges from the fact that he is deprived of it…"

We were having a conversation with Mawlana in our cell. The subject was about Satan. Mawlana asked:

- Is Satan a thing (*shay*) or evil (*shar*)?
- He is unfortunate from the point of love. That is all.

- What was the mystery that he did not prostrate before us?

- It was because he wanted to pass this mystery with you… the sin was committed here… Satan violated the limits… he wanted to go beyond from the place he stayed with angels together with man and wished to regain the peace… It is possible that he refused to prostrate for this reason… like a passionate mad… he was jealous of man… to be in proximity with God… but he did not know that it is impossible to attain Allah without love. That's why he is jealous of humans or in other words, this is the caprice out of frustration for being devoid of love.

- Do you mean that if it is necessary to be human in order to be in proximity with God, then Satan wanted to be a human made of fire?

- Besides the innocent submission of angels, the torrid fire of Satan… It did not know that man can unite fire with light within truth ; had he known that his fire would be in proximity of Allah together with man, do you think that he would prostrate before man?

- We know that Satan's efforts to transform man into fire would be in vain in this world, but if man keeps on fearing God, he would let his Satan to prostrate before him…

- Some people can be the fuel of hell when they die but, Praise be to Lord, they will not be fire in this world… this worldly life is only the mystery on the mirror… the mystery is like the thin film between love and death. Love is the single key for the mystery; and the lock is death. If we can kill the world before dying, there will not be any mysteries in our hearts or in the mirrors… also the Satan that conceals itself in everything… In this way, we can hold Satan from its forelock and let it prostrate before Allah immediately…

- Satan has no power over a person who fears Allah. It only tries to show itself powerful. It never sleeps. However, we save ourselves from it only by remembering Allah continuously. It will be possible then to comply the remembrance (*dhikr*) of Allah in each atom with the unity of the universe in all dimensions. Satan will be destroyed at that moment. You will be among those who are saved. Then, Satan will have no space to live and then will prostrate before man…

- The staff of Moses swallows the serpent…Man's heart lets Satan -who knows no confines – prostrate before Allah… finally the mystery which is hidden even from man himself will be withdrawn… and man leaves the words at the limit and goes beyond *Sidrat al-Muntaha* (The Lote Tree of eternity that marks the end of the seventh Heaven t.n)…

"Oh man who was imprisoned under the shadow of darkness
Realize the light that awaits you within They heart
Which was trusted to you in Paradise
And you were sent to world with that trust
With a light in fire
Then you were crucified within the cross of body
With a blossoming rose in your heart."

Mawlana who missed the Ascension after *halwah*s would find consolation by *sama* in our cell when his feet touched the ground. To attain *mawara* (beyond the visible realm-t.n.) in the journey of soul from space and time.

Each way has its own method
To love God requires a method, too
Dervish does not only mean a wandering Sufi
Whose heart is broad and soul is rich…

We were having a conversation with Mawlana near the roses in the garden of *Dargah.* A group of philosophers came to visit him. They said that they had questions. Mawlana pointed at me:

- Ask your questions to him who answered my questions.

Then they told me that they have three questions. I said,

- Ask your questions, then. They assigned one of them as their spokesperson. He was supposed to ask the questions.

- You say God exists but He is not seen. Show Him and we may believe.

- Ask the other question.

- You say that Satan was created of fire and claim that it will be tormented by fire. How can fire torture fire?

- And your last question?

- You say that everyone will gain their own rewards and be punished for their wrong deeds. Leave them alone that they can do whatever they like.

If that is all, follow me and I will answer your questions. We stood up; we went towards the initiates who were making bricks for the garden wall of *dargah.* I took a dried brick from the ground and hit the man on his head. The philosopher that came to ask a question and those that accompanied him went immediately to *Qadi* of Konya. Mawlana was surprised. I knew what was going through his mind:

Be patient and see how they will come to the *dargah* for repenting after the Qadi's answers. Now, let us pray until the court official calls us to see the Qadi. Almost half an hour later, they called us and we went to the Qadi. The confused philosophers were standing in Qadi's room. The one who I had hit with the brick had had his head bandaged and began telling what had happened:

- I asked a question and he hit me on the head with a brick.

I said:

- I only answered the question.

The Qadi wanted me to explain it.

- He told me to show him Allah in order for him to believe in God. Now tell this philosopher to show his pain so that we may believe in him.

The philosopher was surprised:

- I am in pain but I cannot show it.
- Then Allah exists but He is not visible. In addition, he asked me how Satan will be tormented. I hit him with earth and it hurt his head. However, his body was created from earth, too. And he said leave everyone alone, let them do whatever they wish. I wanted to hit him on the head with the brick and I did. Why did he come here? If one demands his rights even for a small matter in this world, why should we not demand our rights within the life Hereafter which is eternal. The philosopher felt shame after these answers and became silent. He held my hands before everyone:

- I have never seen anyone like you. I asked the same questions to some other Muslim scholars and they uttered thousands of words for hours. I was not satisfied. You are a loyal believer. Make us love Islam.

- Let us return to our uncompleted conversation in our Mawlana's *dargah*. The joy in Mawlana's eyes was visible and he was glorifying me in his horizon of admiration. In order to teach love, you have to establish reliance and then audacity and finally to perfect love. The more I conquered Mawlana, the deeper the ocean became. You have talked with people in the *dargah* and at the mosque so far. Leave them and begin speaking under the firmament! Oh, Mawlana! Arise and Warn (people)! (An allusion to Quran 74:23 t.n) This is the "eleventh hour" for the wicked ones. And the good ones should not feel alone; the love of Allah will occupy all their hearts soon. Satan will no longer come to the heart that prays and includes love.

The fire comes closer with all its heat. It will heat and burn. Who bloweth it? I do not ask Satan but you, Mawlana. I ask about one who wants to be man, one that drinks blood. Who is it? Why doesn't Cain like Abel? Can one know Paradise without seeing Hell? Pity on man.. How can fire be understood without knowing light?

Mawlana: "We could not understand the worth of time. It was a grace given to us to return to Paradise.We were asked to abstain from smokeless fire. We fell either into the center of fire or into cesspit! Oh wicked self"

The white turtledoves withdraw their heads from the darkness of night. The morning flows along with the cold rivers freezing. The night is filled with howling of jackals. A sun is waiting to rise behind the mountain at distance. To rise and to generate. Do you know what it will generate, my dear Mawlana? A Christian Lady will come to your gate with a dead bird in her hands. That dead bird is the self. Blow spirit in it so that it may fly. Let it drink the water of repentance so that it may be Muslim.

Oh *Tannura* (a garment consisted of a large skirt worn by Mawlawi dervishes during Sama-t.n.)! Be the world of hopes, although they break their repenting a thousand times. Gather all tears in your handkerchief those poured during prostration. May the smell of peace occupy the hardened hearts.

Oh, fire! Moisten the oceans. Then the drops should follow you as pearls and corals. Be where there is wickedness, oh Mawlana! Burn Satan's tail. You may collect the dead words from the wicked before they die. Can man know Paradise without seeing hell? The hasty man runs towards hell everywhere. He thinks that light is hastiness. Blood within blood. Fire in fire. Do not let birds drown in the smokeless fire of Satan.

Mawlana begins speaking by a burnt word out of pain. Both of us wish to rush towards Allah. We look at each other and pass through this smokeless fire.

- I do not care about what may happen. Let us go to the peace and cry there; may our tears flow towards eternity like blessed pearls. Mawlana:
- I am exhausted; I am tired in this worldly body. I wish we prayed within the solitary silence and got lost in the spiritual climate.

I told him to stand up. I held his hands and we began whirling together.

- There is no original sin. Satan inscribed this absurdity in the minds and thus covered its wickedness. It is trying to find a partner.
- Could we stay in Paradise without committing the sin? Could we see each other without having to see the other one?

That's why we are on trial. If you have sincerity, you pass the trial. It was in this sense that they called the worldly life

transient. I am the mystery. When the mystery is withdrawn, there will not be any "other".

- Love learns from lust. The reason is that lust means to be the dog of attraction and passion. It generally puts carcass and sometimes fresh meat before you. Those who abstain from passions such as me are called madmen. Praise be to the Lord that I am mad. Thinking has honor and we think in hastiness whereas walking, travelling etc. thought does not depend on pace. When you start thinking, just stop there even if you are in the middle of the street and enjoy thinking for hours. As the soil cannot soak water immediately, the heart also enjoys slow and honorable thought to that extent.
- The morality which is lived unconsciously is not a virtue but incentive imitation.
- All of us have hidden gardens that have plants in them; we are like an old volcano that is almost erupting. If you do not erupt what you have inwardly. Then the outward factors erupt you. Therefore, your garden will be destroyed.
- I will give you poison Jalal al-Din; if you are weak, it will kill you but it will become honey if you are strong enough. Do you accept it?
- I am not a person as such; I am the essence itself.

Mawlana stands and writes something on a piece of paper. He hangs the paper on the door:

- Those who enter here honors me and who do not enter make me happy.
- Seek always the new knowledge. I do not want to see anything that corresponds your former thoughts. Is it my duty to find you new facts?
- Yesterday has gone my dear. Now it is time to say something new.
- Tell me what the "life" is? It is steadily leaving something that wishes to die.
- Is that the only thing I should abstain?

- Of course, not. What does one who abstains do afterwards? He/she tries to attain a higher realm, wants to fly for beyond and highness. He/she gets rid of many things that weigh exceedingly. To throw them is as if you are the soul of a bristle shirt. Begin this task by harming your closest side.
- How and by what?
- Tear the shadow of your 'self'. Drink the water of your soul and get drunk so much that you break your arms and legs on the roads you plunge.

Satan is the knight of spare times that befools everyone saying it eases life and extends lifetime... it is the magnificent dwarf that calls everyone to its smokeless fire. It is the lustful player of fiery words. It is the passionate serpent that envies even the image of paradise trusted to man. It is the blind antichrist that cannot read love.

Those who envy and gossip about us are the ones who are fed by this Satan, oh Mawlana . We speak in love beautifully, carefully in faith regardless of the severe gossiping those satanised ones make. We love and praise Allah, the Owner of love.

"Thou seest the mountains and thinkest them firmly fixed: but they shall pass away as the clouds pass away" (27: 88)

I had to prepare Mawlana for the ascension of the soul during our *Halwah*. Let our body remain still within four walls. Mawlana had to live the station of certainty, "*haqq al-yaqin*" rather than the theoretical aspect of Sufism before being ready to be taken towards the unseen realm. Our Mother Aisha said, "When Mohammed (P.B.U.H) went for his Nocturnal Journey and returned home, his bed was still warm." The body rised and the soul travelled here…

When the preparation for *miraj* (ascension) during *halwah*s was completed, we used to travel in and around the universe. Everybody thought that we were in the cell. However, we were observing them from Heaven.

One night, we disappeared with Mawlana. Kira Hatun (Mawlana's wife) looked for us everywhere in the madrasa but there was no trace of us. Moreover, all the doors were closed. Than Kira Hatun told this event to her son, Sultan Walad, "I was anxious about Mawlana and Tabrizi as they had been staying in the room for three days. That evening was the breaking (*iftar*) time for their fast of attainment. I prepared some food and carried it to their room with Kimya Hatun. We knocked the door. But there was no reply. Kimya knocked the door a few times more. No reply again. I put the tray to the ground and decided to listen to what was happening inside. I heard nothing other than roaring and sounds like those of blowing wind in open fields. "Kimya, probably your father and Shams are not in the room. But where are they?" We left the place. I slept late that night. I was almost asleep when I saw Mawlana praying the Night Prayer. I did not say anything until he finished praying. After the prayer, I realized that he had dust on his feet and his toes were in colorful sand. I asked what had happened in fear. He answered: "there was a sincere dervish who always talked about our love at Kaba. We went there to talk with him. This sand belongs to Hejaz. Keep it and do not tell anyone else". Following that night, I stopped criticizing Shams and understood how profound he is in their *halwah*s. The following day, I told what had happened to my son, Sultan Walad. He said:

- Oh, mother! Do not tell what you have heard or seen. Those who do not know us will make fun of you saying that Kira Hatun was overwhelmed by genies and the one from Tabriz cast a spell on her. The journey of my father and our Pir is not something new.

- All right son. When I took the Indian flower your father gave me under the door to the herbalist in the bazaar, he gave me such a strange answer that I have been in amazement ever since.

- Could you tell me more about that Indian flower?

- One day Mawlana and Shams were in *halwat* in their cell. I was trying to see from the key hole what they were busy with for days without eating or drinking anything inside the room. I saw that Mawlana was sitting opposite of Shams with his knees touching him. I placed my ears on the door due to curiosity about the matter they are talking. Suddenly I saw six majestic men belonging to the unseen realm entering in from the wall of the house. They greeted them, kissed the ground and put a bunch of flowers before Mawlana. They sat there in peace until the noon prayer. They said nothing. After praying the noon prayer, those revered six people raised with a great reverence and went out from the wall again. I fainted due to the greatness of this event. I remained there trembling. They probably realized my trembling behind the door and passed me a bunch of flowers that I had never seen until that day. I heard Shams' voice behind the door: "Sister, these flowers were brought to Mawlana from far away. He thought that you deserve them." I took the flowers to the herbalist. I wanted to learn what they were and where they came from. The herbalists were surprised from the freshness and smell of the flowers. "Where did these rare flowers come from in winter? It grows only in far regions of India and it normally fades before reaching here. What an interesting thing. Do you want to sell it to us?

My servant and I did not believe in what we heard. Now I believe that Shams and your father are observing the world from that cell:

- You see, mother. Shams is so valuable for my father. Shams is a gift for our family and I believe that ones who know him would attain peace gradually.

The first station of the path of love is sharing the same state in *halwat.* Mawlana's wife Kira Hatun who wondered about what we were doing and tried to look inside from the key hole told the disciples and the people who live in the house that we kept silent for hours without uttering a simple world. Those who regard our state as weird should know that the language of love flows from one heart to another without speaking… it is the call of the hearts to each other. At the end of *halwah*, Mawlana said concerning the speech from heart to heart without any words:

- Can thought utter any word unless you stop speaking? You express your thoughts only by speaking. When you stop speaking, they are imprisoned in mind; but when the heart starts speaking, the tongue keeps quiet. I stopped speaking. When he repeated the same sentence, I could not help speaking:

- Be wise and keep quiet! For, the fire of the heart blazes out by self. The flames began breathing. What would you say concerning this matter? Do you want to increase the flames? Their silence sometimes became water or wind for the fire. He stopped speaking. Our silence was in such a state that the sound of our breath reached from cell to the garden and reflected from garden to the cell again.

When we left *halwat*, the puzzled sights of dervishes were mixed with their groaning voices. They were shocked. Everybody was asking each other what the matter was. They had no courage to ask neither Mawlana nor I about what happened there. It was as if the stones of wrath had fallen on them and they were surprised as if the screams exploded their ears.

- Now go and deal with your family. I will sit in the garden for a while.
- It is getting colder and you do not like any garment except that thin coat. Let me send you a robe.
- The one that burns cannot be cold. Go and deal with your family. Then come for the noon prayer.

Come and let me show you how we can play with fire
See if the fire can burn you or you can burn it?

When Mawlana invited me to have dinner with his family, I refused it with my eyes. I was sitting in the garden and looking around as he was having dinner with his family members. A man standing in front of the kitchen door at the *qibla* direction of the garden was acting strangely. This man who did not utter a single word to any person that was going between the garden and the kitchen was looking at me as if we met each other years ago. I asked one of the dervishes:

- Who is that strange man?

The dervish said:

- We call him *Atashbaz* (one who touches ember with bare hands-t.n). He is one of the favorite disciples and dervishes of Mawlana. His real name is Yusuf bin Izz al-Din. He served with great effort and became one of Mawlana's intimate friends due to his love and sincerity. He wanted to cook for Mawlana and the dervishes willingly; and Mawlana accepted his demand.
- Go on. How did he gain the title "*Atashbaz*"?
- One day Yusuf saw that there was no wood in the storage, as he wanted to cook. The service time was soon and it would take longer to provide wood. He went to Mawlana in embarrassment and said "Oh master! There is no wood left in the kitchen. What do you advise me to do? Mawlana

humorously answered, "Put your legs under the pot and boil the water then!" Yusuf effendi entered the kitchen at once and did what Mawlana told him. He cooked the meal by the fire coming out of his toes. Hearing this, Mawlana did not like the unveiling of this miracle and said "what have you done, Oh *Atashbaz*!" Yusuf Izz al-Din was called "*Atashbaz*" (one who plays with fire) since then.

- Where did *Atashbaz* come from and how long has he been under Mawlana's service?
- Neither he nor we know his birthdate and birthplace. As it is said, his childhood was spent in *Laranda* (Karaman, a city near Konya-t.n). He kissed our Master Mawlana's feather coat and wanted to be initiated. Baha al-Din Walad said:
- What do you want to do in our *dargah*? What are you good at?

He said,

- I want to cook meals for you who feed our hearts and also for those who are with you. When Mawlana's father Baha al-Din died, he did not come out of the kitchen and cried for days. Hearing this, Mawlana went to see and tried to console him: oh brother, will you leave us deprived from those delicious meals of yours? Come brother, may our table fill witf rejoice; he gratified him as a member of his family. Atashbaz loves Mawlana so much that he did not want to leave the *dargah*. Thus, he was assigned as the main cook of *dargah*.
- Call him here and let us see what he learnt from Mawlana.

The dervishes brought *Atashbaz* there.

- Did you have *wudu (ablution)*?
- I never take a step without *wudu*?
- Bring me some water for ablution, but it should be cold.

He went away and brought an ewer with him. As he was pouring water, I realized that the water was boiling that it almost scalded my hands.

- What on earth are you doing man? Did not I tell you to bring cold water? Do you want to burn my hands?
- Forgive me master, I put the water especially from the fountain.
- What do you mean, am I a liar?

I shouted at him and called two dervishes.

- Pour some water from the ewer.

They did. Then I asked:

- How was the water?
- Cold as ice… our fingers were almost frozen.

As Atasbaz watched us in astonishment, he blushed out of shame. I told the dervishes to leave there. Then I said.

- Tell me player of fire, what is the difference between the prayer of lovers and that of scholars?
- The canonical prayers of scholars who illuminate and guide people are five times a day. However, the lovers pray all the time.
- Have you ever ridden the horse of repentance that takes its owner from ground to the heavens at a single moment?

I told that stranger who plays with fire:

- Take me to your fire. We went near the oven in the kitchen. When I told him that I wanted to see how he plays with fire, he suddenly leaned into the oven. The flames covered his face. Some reddish shadows appeared on his beard. A trace of an old gleam was seen in his eyes.

I repeated "love is to be burnt in fire". The fire approved, it showed its blazing tongue towards wood. The wood understood it and withdrew suddenly. The water that prevented the first attempt of fire fell into the ember and vapored. At the second attempt, the body of wood turned into red and its pores were filled with smoke. It began crying.

- Will you tell what you have seen to others?
- I uttered only three words.

He looked into my eyes.

- Only three words? You told us about the world you come from. You spoke inside that world. You spoke too much and made us tired. You shouted while whispering. The words were not from your flesh. When you said, "love is to burn in fire", you showed being here at the time of death as proof. I put my finger on his lips:

- Speak with your state and speak to your friend as usual. If I had not witnessed the play of fire with love, you would have been sent from the *dargah* today. Well done, you passed my trial. Now, I may eat from your soup. Bring me a bowl of soup and a loaf of dry bread once every three days after evening prayer. I want no other food.

When I left the kitchen, I met Mawlana. He was looking in curiosity. I said:

- Those who are around you deserve trial. Be patient until your turn. *Atashbaz* passed the trial. Is it possible to pick grapes from thorny bushes and figs from thistles? *Atashbaz* has already drunk from fire. Let us pray now.

Probably you wonder why I put Mawlana's relatives and people around him on trial. In order to polish a light, you cannot blow your wind without knowing whether the things around it are dark walls or deaf veils.

One day Mawlana told about my greatness and proximity to Allah at full length to the members of his family and wanted them not to hesitate in showing respect to me and ask about my condition at times. After all these words, his son Sultan Walad came into my cell, kissed my hand and served me. I could not understand the reason for this sudden visit and said:

- Walad, what has happened to you? You show excessive respect and affection in order to please me.

- Sir, my father told us so much about you that we got mad. If I had a thousand years of lifetime, and served you continuously and knew all my service was accepted, there would be a great frustration within me making me doubt whether I have done enough or not.

- That's kind of Mawlana; hundreds of thousands of Shams are nothing more than an atom compared with his greatness. Although I attained intuitions (*mukashafa*), observed the sultans of spiritual journey, became in proximity with divine lights, lived many spiritual man and see the unseen realms, I could not reach Mawlana. Now, who can attain his truth?

- Your father is an ocean. Do not let its water recede, son. Guard your brother Alaaddin. He is not as humble as you are, he would put Mawlana in trouble. He is together with some wicked people. He plunged into the water of Satan that is politics and lost his conscious. Due to the bluntness of his youth, he will put himself in trouble.

It is a great bliss given by Allah to be able to see your face. One who wants to see Prophet Mohammed should go and see Mawlana. He should prostrate before him with ease like the grass that sways by winds. One who wants to live just the opposite may live as he wishes.

Blessed is one who finds Mawlana. Who am I?... I found him and I am happy, too. If you have belief, remove your doubts.

I want to speak only with Mawlana, not with anyone else. Come nearer and I will say something into your ears. I want to do something; but if Allah does not will, he will not listen to me. One who sees us becomes either a greater Muslim or a severe disbeliever. For, those who could not realize our spirituality see only the outward and find imperfectness in our worshipping only outwardly. They think that his rank is high and he has no need for worshipping. They become distant from worshipping, the reason for real loyalty of worlds.

FROM "JALAL AL-DIN" TO "MAWLANA"

You were scholar and became a sage, are you a candidate for love?
You are not a poet. A poet transmits the public what he gained from them.
However, the lover presents public what he gained from the All-Truth

People are curious mostly on the following: How is it that a person, who remained as *Jalal al-Din* despite the experience of forty years, transformed into *Mawlana* in forty days? What did Shams do within those forty days and that raw one became ripen? The mystery was in our *halwah.* Only the ripen ones know how to take a wise person to Divine love. It was I who could fulfill this task and it was only I who saw Mawlana as he was.

Can one know paradise without seeing hell? The hasty man rushes toward hell from all directions. Pace… Pace is a mystery. The pace of blood and that of fire cannot reach the pace of light. Only the heart that is covered with light understands who the angel is and who the devil is. We are surrounded by the flames. No one is aware of the fact that he/she is burning. I had flames to burn him in my *halwah.*

Do you wonder about the effect of *halwah*? You should come side by side in order to reach *halwah.* To stand together in rows. To be attached to paradise beginning from that moment. We need to put all priorities aside and talk about how our counsels on intimate knowledge would influence the descendants of Satan. Even if we lose our body to find the meaning of heart, the help of our heart is enough to keep our mind pure. All our minds were a river flowing towards paradise before they came to the world. Divine love was trusted only to us, to the heart.

The worldly life does not last even a moment. When you touch your forehead to the earth smiling as if you saw Allah in silence in the stone courtyard with the sound of water coming from the fountain and as the sunlight casts on your face, a gentle breeze blows at that very moment. The scents of roses spread all around the courtyard. Moreover, you feel yourself praying together with our Prophet in *Rawdha*, in *Masjid al-Nabawi*.

The worldly life comes to end at that time. Time, space, man cease to exist. You wake up before your Lord in the primordial state. All secrets will be unveiled for you. You become a secret and return to the world.

The owner of Divine love allowed us for this love. I said we, both of us, would not be able to go beyond the seventh Heaven (*Sidrat al-Muntaha*), Oh Lord, to come to you; we would be burnt… we would be like angels but could not come nearer to you. We are in the world again. We could be like angels but would not be able to come nearer to you. Now, we are in the world in daily life: but in such a state that is closest to you. We are in *halwah* in canonical prayers and prostrations. With our repenting. We are closing our doors to the world. We are in *halwah* again. We closed the doors and opened our hearts to the windows of the nocturnal journey of love. We do not open that door to anyone that knocks it. We say we are not there; we do not exist. We used to exist but now we are nonexistent. There is no Mawlana, no Shams. No one exists there. We left our hearts at that moment. We are ascending. The scent of our Prophet and his light is in Heaven. The secret of the secrets… the gate of heavens is opening now. We move from one state to another. We are in an ocean of words. The letters are bowing down; at first, "*aliph*" and then "*nûn*" and others. The words become ways for us. Mawlana remains silent. We are in a time that has no future. There is nothing that is nonexistent. It is only Allah who exists. Nothing existed in the world. It was only an allusion. The intellect thought it could know everything. It could not know it. It could not know even itself. We are in the heart again.

- Is it possible to love without considering death?
- Are not love and death a single word in reality?
- Then what is that world they are waiting for, which world is sought in such yearning?
- Death and love. The two journeys towards Allah, the secret lies here: In the heart and together with the light of Muhammad.

Oh, the first word that remained in light! We saw you in "*Heaven*". All words we uttered before you were in vain. We understood this fact. We renewed our heart. Our face was overwhelmed with light. When we looked at each other's face, we saw "Him" in our hearts; we saw the light of mystery… the voice and the world. We came down to Konya with this gift.

"The Earth, Heaven, Nocturnal Journey, Light, Mystery, Love" "Allah has seventy veils of light. If He had unveiled them, the greatness of His face would have burnt everything that the eyes of the creation perceived. The only key to open the seventh door: Love …

I say "How majestic you are (*subhanaka*).The meaning of *subhanaka* is as follows: if your heart is inclined to beauty, He says, "The perfect beauty is here"; if your heart is inclined to properties, He says, "The perfect Richness is here". If it is inclined to the rank, He says, "The best rank is here". If it is inclined to *Sama* and to the speech of other people, He says, "The perfect Mercy and Bliss is here". All the qualities are as such that He says, "It is I who protect and observe", that is to say, a hen cannot protect its chicks as I save my friends. All these are for lest you say, "Allah does not love me. He does not estrange me for the taste of His beauty". You cannot find the sweetness that comes from Allah from any other merciful protector.

Subhanaka. Allah says, "Nothing you love or seek is perfect". The supreme Lord says, "Place love here, as I am pure and perfect".

At any time, I have the ardent movement of Jesus, the ecstasy of Moses, the Certainty of Mohammad (P.B.U.H), the intuition and perseverance of saints, the sweet happiness of lovers together with the beauty of the beloved.

The happiness of visible world is revived by the happiness of unseen world. The unseen world finds revival from the qualities of Allah. Then the gates opening to the eternal garden whose name is "paradise" are the attributes of Allah and a door is opened in all kinds of happiness in the world so that He gives joy and develops it. Now come and let us give ourselves to those gates of Allah and enter into Paradise; to the extent not to remember the world any longer; but let us remind and remember Allah and let us submit ourselves to Him.

I was invoking Allah. I said, "How can I love Allah unless He loves me? A kind of love that is one sided is impossible. One hand does not sound. Likewise, the inclination of *houries* towards the residents of paradise is the divine love. It was as if Allah embraces us at first just as two forms embrace each other; this is the love of two souls. However, there is no such embracing at the level of the reality of soul and the meaning of form.

Many Sufis read Quran as a letter from their beloved; in this respect, although the lover sometimes utters bitter words to warn their hearts, they interpret It in an optimistic manner.

Is it right to adopt a religion in that Allah enjoins it, to be safe from punishment, or to be able to enter the Paradise? Of course not. As the efficiency of God is motivated by His love towards humanity, human behavior should be motivated by divine love.

Oh my dear Mawlana, let me speak and you will listen; let me keep silent and you will overflow. Let us start from our father Adam for the love of *halwah*:

When Allah wanted to explain to Adam that he had to leave Paradise, He said:

"Jewels and black stones shine forth in your cup of existence. Pearls and the broken pieces of pots are hidden in the ocean of nature. We have two homes: we set the table of feast of beautiful pleasures on one and trusted it to *Ridwan*(angel). And we lit the fire of wrath in the other and trusted it to *Malik* (angel). If we had allowed you to stay in the garden, our name *Qahhar* (one who gives wrath) would not have been satisfied with it. Then leave here, go into the furnace of grief and the pot of distance. We will unveil the trusts, arts, pearls, and duties hidden in your heart afterwards...

The Bliss and Wrath of Allah are reflected in two dimensions of Adam: "soul" and "clay". If it had not been the wrath of clay, Adam would have been an angel, not human; and he would not have been the vicegerent of Allah.

If there had been only the soul, his days would have been purified from defects and his deeds would not have been all mixed up ; but pure works are not appropriate for this world. And I added that Adam was created as vicegerent for this world initially. Mawlana said:

- If Adam had stayed in Paradise, would not he been a vicegerent?

Adam was not thrown from paradise because of a small fault. Even if we accept that he had not committed that small fault, he would have been brought down again. The reason of his coming is that the caliphate (vicegerent) and the carpet of sultanate were waiting for his steps. Ibn Abbas said, "Allah has taken Adam out of the Paradise before he entered there".

Adam has two existences: the first and the second existence. The first existence belongs to this lower world, not to the paradise. and the second one belongs to the paradise. "Oh Adam, leave the paradise and enter this world. Leave your crown, belt and turban on the path of love! Be exposed to troubles. We will give you this valuable realm again, in a hundred thousand garments of bliss and all kinds of honor as the leader of witness before those hundred and twenty thousand prophets who are the sources of excellence and the owners of purity. The creation following him will know that We may bring the body of Adam by the name of Bliss as We had taken him out of paradise by the attribute of wrath."

Adam will enter the paradise with his descendants later on. A scream will arise from each corner of paradise due to the crowdedness. The angels of Angelic Realm will look at them in amazement and say, "Isn't he the one who was taken out the paradise a few days ago?

"Adam, to take you from the paradise was a veil over the secrets; for, your lucky descendants were the ocean of more than a hundred and twenty thousand pearls of Prophethood. Endure for a little and then attain the treasure within a few days!"

The Divine Love gives answers to all His Names. Angels are deprived of Love; they cannot taste perdition, wrath and distance; likewise, animals are far from love; for, they cannot experience beauty, mildness and proximity. Human beings are woven by proximity and distance, bliss and perdition. All opposite divine attributes united in them. Only Allah in whom all opposites united can love them. "Within the eighteen thousand worlds, it is only human beings who drank from the cup that is full of the idea that Allah may love them."

- Adam showed disobedience to Allah by His encouragement; for, Allah knew that Adam would not conceive the attributes of distance, which will enable Adam to be a lover without disobedience. The essence of love is yearning and sorrow.

- Our Lord who prevented *Yusuf* (Joseph) from committing a bad act could have saved Adam from tasting that fruit; however, the world should have been filled with chaos, grief and troubles.

- When Allah burdened that trust to heavens, earth and mountains, all of them rejected it. For, they did not know the mystery of love; but Adam thought only of the Beloved. Thus, he was not uncomfortable seeing his incompetence despite the fact that the trust was such a heavy burden, which all creation feared.

- My dear Mawlana, the sign of lovers is yearning; they desire only the beloved. They have to purify their inward from everything in the universe even from the paradise in order to attain it.

- Adam had longing in him. He was busy with his yearning. When man attains something, he does this by yearning. Otherwise, he cannot attain anything with only what he has in his very being.

- So, what makes Adam great is the concept that he carried the trust which is divine love. He only knew the mystery of love; for, the love was the reason lying beneath its *raison d'etre*. He knew that his love would be strengthened only when he tasted the pain of separation. He ate from the forbidden fruit for this reason.

- My dear friend from Tabriz, why did those who could not understand our father Adam transform the universe into the sin of blood?

- They experienced this condition because they looked at the sun of hope as their eyes were closed.

- Who closed the eyes of human beings?

- The robbers of hope.

- How?

- "Say: "O my Servants who have transgressed against their souls. Despair not of the Mercy of God: for God forgives all sins: for He is Oft-Forgiving, Most Merciful." (Quran, 6:53)

It was narrated that a person recited this verse before the Messenger of Allah. When he was reading the part "God forgives all sins", The Holy Prophet said "He surely will" and said "Allah curses those who put people into hopeless from divine Mercy" three times.

According to accounts, Prophet Moses said, "Oh Allah, Why do You want disobedience from your servants although You do not like it". Allah said, "In order to fulfill My forgiveness."

- What if one asks, "Despite all the honor and supremeness bestowed over humanity, why did Allah decree to test them by disobedience?"

My dear Mawlana, this question has many answers. Firstly, the underlying wisdom here is that the servant should not be overwhelmed by pride; for, pride invites the veil. Don't you see that *Balam* became a dog when he (*Balam*, Pharaoh's leading scholar on religious sciences –t.n) claimed the Supreme Name for himself (7:176).

He was the master of hearts and authority; but then became worse than a dog because of those vain desires.

Another answer: the art, aptitude and mastery of a glass-maker becomes apparent a broken glass. Your heart is like glass. The stone of rebel stroke and broke it. The Lord of Bliss reunites it by the fire of penitence: "without doubt, I am (also) He that forgives again and again, to those who repent, believe, and do right, who, - in fine, are ready to receive true guidance"(20:82). Although He said to you Moses "Verily, I am Allah. There is no god but I" (20:14) in his case of majesty, He said to us "I am (also) He that forgives again and again"

Yet another answer: Allah has two storages; one full of reward and the other one full of forgiveness and mercy. "If you obey Me, you will have plenty of rewards and gifts. But if you disobey, you will find mercy and forgiveness. Thus, my storage is not in vain…

-Allah says, "I will forgive them all". He says "I will forgive", not "I forgave" lest the servant would leave supplications, fear and hope. The servant should remain between fear (*hawf*) and hope (*raja*); supplicate continuously and pray fervently to God. "…O ye Believers! Turn ye all together towards Allah, that ye may attain Bliss"(24: 31) "Say: "O my Servants who have transgressed against their souls! Despair not of the Mercy of Allah: for Allah forgives all sins: for He is Oft-Forgiving, Most Merciful. (39:53)

Oh my servants! Which servants? Not "those who obey", or "who reply", or "who pray their canonical prayers" or who perform hajj", or "who perform jihad" or "who give alms". Then who? Those who go beyond the limits, who transgressed.

- You interpreted "those who transgressed" very well, Mawlana. He did not remove the veil. He did not say, "They committed adultery, they killed. In short, He said "those who transgressed". They were excessive. He forgives as He wills. He did not remove the veil.

He neither called the highest Heaven as "Oh my *Lawh*"; neither Paradise as "Oh my Paradise" and fire as "Oh my fire".

He called the rebels as "Oh my servants". This suffices you as an honor.

On the day of Judgement, you will say "my body". Prophet Mohammed will say "My followers" (*ummah*). Paradise will say "my portion" and Hell will say "my part". The Lord of Bliss will say "My servant".

MY MAWLANA

There is no "above" or "below" in love
Then why should I seek for more?
I am also like love itself.

We were fond of each other, we were observing each other; our mutual teaching continued for days regardless of who the teacher and the pupil was. We were illuminating the entire universe and the flowing rivers into the hearts in a cell whereas a world without spirit was boiling intensely.

As Mawlana, who was admired by the people in Konya and whose preaching was listened with utmost care, disappeared and left the disciples and his madrasa suddenly surprised everyone at first; then this surprise turned into fear. They left Mawlana alone for a while but rumors began a few months later. Those fanatic groups could not understand why Mawlana, whom they spent their time together, left all worldly affairs by means of following me about whom they have no sufficient knowledge and for whom they had many unanswered questions. The excessive admiration they had for Mawlana led them to envy.

- What is the meaning of all these? Who is this person that makes Mawlana busy with himself and reserves him from all his old fellows? Where did he come from and what does he want to do? And sometimes they went too far in their actions.

They gradually proclaimed these utterances of mischief, which they could not pronounce before and began even bothering me.

One day as I was walking in the streets of Konya, a few men gave some money to children and sent them to tease me. When the children were just intending to throw pebbles at me, I turned back suddenly and they stopped thereof. I think a kind of spiritual power showed me in such a state that they put the pebbles down and kissed my hands. What made me sad was that those who sent them could not be as innocent as these children. I went into a shop and wanted a needle and some thread. He forced me to go out cursing, "Oh mad man, you came and destroyed our Master. You also pierced our hearts. Go away". As I was leaving the shop, I took a glance at him. The stone building collapsed as soon as I left the shop.

Until I learnt a single page on your love
I forgot a hundred pages on other sciences.

I was a dilemma for everyone in Konya. Who I was and why I was there? What did I do to Mawlana to keep silent as such? What was my strength on transforming his world? Did I cast magic on Mawlana? Why were they so hopeless against my anger? They were angry with me but were afraid of me at the same time. They were growing their prejudice and could not help their whims concerning my personality. The questions in their minds were increasing in number day by day. Let them remain in their curiosity…I had a friend who could understand me. If you gather those who know Jalal al – Din, you would see how few they were; but I will make him Mawlana and present him to the entire world. If Jalal al-Din, who was living just like a simple civil servant, went on living in tins, he would become rusty. I would polish that diamond and say, "he is jewel and his place is the entire world, not these streets". We needed time. I had to train him slowly. I did not care what they thought or said. The tombstones or blind walls would produce mere roaring even if they spoke. Let me leak some water through the rocks of Konya so that Rose-cheeked remove its aridness.

Mawlana used to read the *Diwan* (collection of poem s- t.n) of *Mutanabbi* in the evenings with great ardor.

- Do not read that book of *Mutanabbi,* what do you find in those dry poems? He did not pay attention to my words. The following evening, he took the same book. I cast a glance;

we looked at each other. I made a wry face. He put *Diwan* on the cushion and went to his bedroom to sleep next to his wife. The following morning, he rushed into my room in unease.

- We need to go to the masjid.

- It is not the time for prayer yet.

- Not for the Morning Prayer.

- Then for which prayer?

- The prayer of fear.

- What has happened?

- In my dream, you were holding *Mutanabbi*'s ear and brought him here. You were shouting and saying "Are you reading his words?" Poor *Mutanabbi* was trembling and said, "Save me from Shams and do not be busy with my book any longer". I smiled and said,

- Was there any need for a warning from the world of dreams in order to stop you from reading those?

I was preparing to sleep one night. I heard something in front of my door. It was as if someone was inscribing something on my door – or maybe repairing it. I did not pay attention and slept. When I woke up in the morning, I saw Mawlana sleeping in front of my door. He rose suddenly. I saw that it was written "The place of Khidr's beloved" in red on the door. I blew the inscription and it disappeared. I said,

"Once you realize that he deluded me with gold and silver. Then he deluded me with fame and rank. However, we have left that rank and fame for so long."

He was embarrassed. I put my hands on his shoulder. He was happy when I offered to teach him *sama*.

Oh, Jalal al-Din! If you demand my heart
Devote your loneliness to me.

Not only the public but also Mawlana was anxious about what was happening. His way of life changed day by day. He was curious. He was under the effect of Shams on one hand and could not help removing whims in his mind on the other. I cannot fire the love without removing what you have in your mind. Ask me what you want to.

- You have a breath just as that of Jesus.

- And?

- You have no equivalent in the science of alchemy.

- Possible. What else?

- You have great competence in sciences such as astrology, geometry, theology, philosophy, interpretation of Quran, tradition of Holy Prophet, etc. How is this possible? You never had an education at school or stayed at *dargah*, and had no master. How did you gain all these?

- I established my state of heart. Is there any other master more skillful than the heart? I was tired of searching for years. Then I realized that what I sought was in me and what I found was in you. Did our Prophet have a school education?

- No.

- Did he know to write and read?

- No.

- Then why was he in the cave?

...

Let me tell ... the wall was Joseph's school. The desert was Jesus and Moses' *dargah*. The cave was Mohammad's school of heart. Do you think that knowledge comes only from the books and a teacher? It is possible that sometimes a camel can tell something that tens of volumes cannot explain. Allah says in the Quran, "Don't you look at a camel...?"

Then what should be read from a camel? Mawlana, this is where your rawness lies. You are dependent on books. The universe is also a book. Prophet Mohammad was a walking book. Just read the lines of books of trees, fire and water. Mawlana's face became pale.

- I have a question but I have to put these trusts into this chest for good. He stood up and took several storybooks from by the window. He opened the walnut chest; he kissed the books and then placed them in it. He turned towards me and said,

- How did you choose the world of isolation, unity and discernment after removing the intellectual and religious science by a single stroke of pen despite your mastery in them?

- The answer is in you. You also thought once that your father's book, the gift of Farid al-Din Attar and other books were indispensable for you. You renunciated them at once just as I chose the realm of unity.

People have surprised me ever since I saw them as simply flesh and bones. One day I was sitting by the front gate of madrasa. Although the other parts of the garden were shady I chose to sit cross-legged on a stone. Everywhere was blue, green, yellow and white; the only black thing was the coat I was wearing. I was in seclusion (*uzlah*). I did not want to be bothered by any voice. In the meantime, a huge person was passing by; he was a executioner. A few curios men were standing close by. The executioner pointed at me and said to the others:

- This man is a saint.
- I was silent.

He repeated the same sentence. I heard but remained silent whereas I was screaming from within "Go away man, do not unveil our state." I was silent. As the man kept on repeating the same sentence, the crowd grew bigger. I realized that he was not thinking of leaving thus my seclusion would be ruined. I waited for him to repeat that sentence.

- This man is a saint.

A man among the people could not help speaking and told what he thought.

- This man is the executioner of Mawlana. I raised my voice:
- Yes, I am either a saint or a madman. I am a saint in that I saved Mawlana from the dungeon of the body and cage of matter. And I am mad in that I would not unveil the mystery. Now everybody leave.

I was attracting the relatives of Mawlana as I attracted him. If you love and wish goodness for Mawlana, you need to make his friends happy and conquer them. *Ahi Husam al-Din* who did not like me at the beginning and approached me with care was one of them. During the Morning Prayer, Mawlana was imam, Husam al-Din was the *muadhin*; I, Sultan Walad and other disciples were the congregation behind the imam (*jamaah).* Husam al-Din who stood up for *qamah* (the call for obligatory prayer, ie *fardh*), suddenly fainted with my smile. They took him to his room. I visited him after the prayer.

- Get well soon, oh brother. You passed the trial by a single glance. He rose and kissed my hand. He said,
- I did not like you much. Forgive me. I am ready to fulfill whatever you wish.

"Oh Husam al-Din! In accordance with "Spend for the sake of religion", give something and show piety so that you approach us.

Husam al-Din went home immediately. He brought whatever he found including money, dishes and even garments; and put them before me. He had a vineyard in Gilistra village, which was like a garden in paradise. He sold it and brought the money. He was praying and praising God that a sultan honored him by wanting such things from him.

- Yes, Husam al-Din. I hope from the divine Bliss, the help of his servants so much that you will attain a state desired by the most ripen ones, and you will be a person that your pure brothers admire. Although the friends of God are in need of nothing, they are not poor and secluded from both worlds; the admired person is tested firstly by leaving the love of lover and the world; and secondly by leaving everything other than Allah. The disciple that desires much never finds way to what he sought; he finds way only to eating much and servitude. The verse in which it is said, "Who gives, fears Allah and abstains wickedness" is the sign on the flag of the Greatest Loyal (Abu Bakr). Those who are loyal and truthful should be like *Abu Bakr as-Siddiq*. Each disciple and lover who spends his wealth on their Master's path can sacrifice his head. The lovers who are purified from all kinds of hypocrisy and who believe sincerely are almost extinct."

Take this bag full of gold coins! In accordance with the verse "Give Allah a loan", come forth. If you spend a single coin, then you will gain a hundred thousand coins as a reward.

I took only a dirham among all those goods and money Husam al-Din put before me. I gave the rest to Husam al-Din and glorified him to an inexpressible extent. Husam al-Din attained such a state that those whose eyes of the heart are open put their heads on his chest. Mawlana used to call him as "The keeper of Heavenly treasures."

If Allah will revive a person by your hands
How will not you give your hand? Allah wants you to be admired by people
And He collects your dispersed parts.
Do not show ingratitude for love!

Those who saw us could not differentiate who the master and who the disciple was. As the veils withdrawn, the fog of language and the visible borders are burnt, we wake up from another sleep; we sleep again and again…

They invited me to a circle in Konya; the aim here was to bring a madman (*majdhub*) and let that madman to put me to shame. They made their plans. I arrived and they wanted me to sit on a cushion on the left. I sat on the cushion. I looked at the people in that room. There were some leading merchants of Konya, scholars of madrasa and a few Sufis. After greeting each other, the madman who was warned prior stood up and said:

- *Efendi* (sir), I heard that you are a clear-sighted, clever master who knows the secrets. I have a problem: I lost my donkey that was the only thing I had. Tell me where it is in Konya. Please help me find it.
- Sit down for a while, I will find your donkey soon. Now tell me, oh friends, is there anyone who does not know what love is or is there anyone who has not experienced love before? They looked at me in surprise. Then they lowered their heads and began thinking. They were silent. One of them stood up and said:

- Right, I do not really know how to love someone. Two other people answered in the same manner and I turned to the madman who wanted to learn where his donkey was:
- Look, you lost one donkey but I found three donkeys for you.

THE WIND OF RESURRECTION BURNS THE STREETS OF KONYA

Hu. Have you ever seen a lover who is satisfied with this love?
Have you seen any fish satisfied with the sea in which lives and swims?

The easiest thing those societies, who fear facing with their fears, manage to do is to curse love. For, the society is against the realization of supreme love. How can those who think Sufism consists only of form know you, oh love? The real Muslim does not fear love. Although Mawlana was in such a tiring effort to show the right way to the community, the seekers understood him in the following centuries, rather than his own period. What a strange contradiction! As the time passed, the gossiping and jealousy increased. The public had nothing to deal with other than wickedness. Everyone was gossiping. The words went out of closed doors and lived in the streets. The men were talking about me in the courtyard of the mosque and in front of the shops; the women were gossiping during their counsels in their houses and at the bazaar. Their grumbling would increase as I was passing before them. They were expressing their poisonous words shouting as if I killed the essence of community. They were practicing all kinds of revilements. When Mawlana was informed about these bitter words, a painful smile was seen on his face and he told them the following in tears:

- Your opinions concerning Shams are out of your dislike for him. If you loved him as I did, you would push each other in order to kiss his feet. You even could not do what the women did when they saw prophet Joseph. Shame on you!

I arrived in Konya months ago. Mawlana did not go to his madrasa as he did before and I did not allow him to see anybody else except his family members. His days started with me and his nights commenced with me too. The love of Allah should, of course, be dominant over gossiping. He was a diamond; he had nothing to do with tins. Alaaddin, who was energetic and had a sharp tongue as mine and who had a piercing sight entered my room immediately after his father left there one morning:

- Oh you stranger bandit, whose garment and tongue is black! What do you want from our Mawlana?
- First, you entered my room without permission. Secondly, you did not greet. Thirdly, I have a name. As to your problem, why did those so called clever men provoke you to come here?
- I would not have left without slaughtering you if my father had not had love for you.
- Stop speaking nonsense. You show your teeth like mad dogs, but you do not have an intention to bite me.
- You stole my father. You are mad.
- I did not take anyone from anybody. In addition, I am not mad. I am mad for a saint, that's all. Your father is a friend of Allah, not yours. The friends of Allah are the saints of Him. Now be wise and leave my room. Tell those who sent you here that I would destroy them. I will give my head for the sake of your father, as they will not make any movement when the time comes.

Although some underestimated me and considered me unimportant, I did not care. It is strange that some call me saint. Supposing this is true, what pride do I have from it? If I am proud of it, it is something unpleasant; however, Mawlana is a saint as it is understood from the qualities mentioned in the Quran and the tradition of the Prophet. I am a friend of a friend, saint of a saint; from this respect, I am loyal to you.

Mawlana completed his own madrasa and established a great circle. Those scholars were discussing a where the head place (*sadir)* was. I was a new comer to Konya those days. Mawlana was sitting on the lowest place among them. They asked Mawlana where the *sadir* was. He said "The place (*sadir*) of scholars is the middle of the room. The place of the sages is at the corner of the room. The place of Sufis is at the sides of the room. For the Lovers, the place is next to the friend." He stood up immediately and sat next to me. Mawlana's behavior would cause them to show envy towards me. I was glad for this action. I did not care about anyone else except for the friend. Mawlana loves me even more than his own soul and does not approve of a single nail to be hammered on the wall of my room. He said if you hammer a single nail on Shams' wall, it will pierce my body."

Most of the disciples consisted of men who were very much despised. The people around him had low incomes, were poor, committed crimes and came out of prison recently and had almost no education. Mawlana answered those who criticized his followers, "if they consisted of good people, I would be their disciple. I initiated them to enable them to change their morality and be good, and to enter among those who commit good deeds. Those who attained divine mercy are saved. However, they were exposed to curses and are in need of healing. We came to this world only to make those cursed ones to be among who were bestowed mercy." He became greater in my heart by this very answer. Other so-called spiritual masters were fools that tried to gain fame around sultans, begged and became rich. They were competing in good eloquence. Mawlana was my eagle who flew towards the summit by his maturity and who tried to pierce the clouds.

Now, I want to explain the incident when Mawlana said, "I am hurt". They said, "Shams profits from Mawlana's words". Of course, he gives me clues on some certain subjects; but they are not for you; they are for me. Look! He found me as a stranger and let me attain comfort and peace. Then who does Mawlana belong to? He does not leave whom he chooses. Each of his dreams is realized in the morning and its effect goes on until noontime. How is it possible? Is this a different sort of prayer? I tried sincerely for this fact not to become a habit. By Allah, to see your face is sacred! One who wants to see Prophet Mohammed should go and see Mawlana without hesitation. One who rejects it is one who does not know how to live. Blessed is one who finds Mawlana. Who am I? I am one of those who found him. If you have any doubt in your belief, he will remove those doubts. The reason for the creation of both worlds is the meeting of two friends. These two friends should meet without any ostentation or any kind of ambition for the sake of Allah. There should not be problems like bread, bakery and butcher. I am so glad now in the presence of Mawlana.

Oh Mawlana, who is a lover! You do not need any praise. Oh people, stop praising him. Praising should comfort him and make him happy (but this is not the case in reality). Do not pronounce anything to hurt his heart and make him unhappy. Whatever makes me unhappy also makes him unhappy.

Mawlana and my personal features are completely different. I have such a nature that I may utter vulgar words when I am angry due to my sharp tongue and that I never hesitate to offend people and my disciples whereas Mawlana exerts his criticism in a manner not to offend people, utters gentle words, and has a nature that is merciful towards all human beings and animals. Mawlana never gave up showing mercy and tenderness even for the aim of teaching. This feature of him is rather due to his nature. Mawlana's face is beautiful. We have both good and ugly sides. Mawlana saw our good side, not the bad one. Now, I do not want to be hypocrite and hide my bad side, he should see me as I am so that he may understand not only the good side but also the bad one.

- Mawlana is the moon. Eyes cannot reach the sun of my being; they can only reach the moon. The eyes cannot look at the sun due to its blinding radiance. The moon cannot reach the sun but the sun can reach it. As it is stated in the Quran, "The eyes cannot conceive Him but He conceives them."

There are some certain words from divine knowledge in Mawlana. He does not think whether his words are profitable for others; but I have a state inspired by Allah since my childhood. If I train someone by words, he would be saved from his own being.

I looked for myself in you
I lost you in me, why then
Should I seek more, however,
I am just like you.

Mawlana's face is beautiful; mine is (it depends to the person) both good and bad. Mawlana saw my good side, not the bad one. I will not commit any hypocrisy now and will unveil both sides.

Whoever participates in my circle finds the circles of others rather boring and unpleasant. In this case, he does not communicate with them willingly due to this unpleasant state.

They said, "Mawlana is a diver and I am a merchant. We have a jewel among us." "Let the path of that jewel give a way to us among you."

I said "Yes, but the true way is as follows: I do not say that give me something. I mean 'what is the right way leading to Allah' by the language of that inner state and the intention of supplication. Let me explain the way to Allah: if you want to go to Aksaray, there is a bridge to pass over on the way. It is called "they strive with their wealth and lives". Firstly, you should pass it by sacrificing your belongings and soul; then you have a lot to do. If it is necessary to go to Aksaray, there is no way apart from that path and bridge. The path goes through deserted plains. You will lose your way there. The monsters and troubles (ghouls) shoot ahead their own places.

They accompany but then absorb you. Now tell me, what will you do? What will you sacrifice? Tell me what you have in your heart sincerely. If you have an obstacle, tell me plainly, so that I will try to remove it. For, I know that path better than you do.

I am talking about a jewel but you do not spend a penny for it! Should I be a hypocrite or tell you the truth? Mawlana is the moon; eyes cannot endure my sun like being. The moon cannot reach the sun but the sun can reach the moon. As it is stated in Quran, "The eyes cannot conceive it but we conceive what the eyes see."

I was able to remove the dust on the jewel that I would process and display it. The dust of the jewel was esoteric and exoteric knowledge gained until that time.

I removed from Mawlana whatever he had concerning the past. I decided to remove everything he gained until that time. For, I would clothe him with the veil of love. Actually, Mawlana abstained worldly things following my instructions. He gave up preaching and teaching in the madrasa. He stopped communicating with people. He said:

"Yesterday has gone with yesterday my dear

With all that belongs to past

Now, it's time to say something new."

He became my initiate with full submission. For, submission and contentment is the merit of brave ones.

I also lead a life as I recommended him. I have never given importance on any laws, authority or wealth in my life. I entered this path in order to transform the rules into a reverse manner. I never had the fear of "what people think about me". I recommended Mawlana to be deaf towards the outside world.

THE EXILE OF LOVE

Go now, oh loyal one! Do not let the lips of those who seek wicked words open; do not let them make use of your words for gossiping.
Do not tell them that you are in search of me and let them call you a lunatic.
Go now before anybody sees you here. Know it well that I exist and you are in me.

My influence on Mawlana caused jealousy and malice. Moreover, this fire of incitement made Konya a field of fire. I was cooking Mawlana over the fire of light and made the public exploded by the fire of language without paying attention to what was being said. One day, Mawlana was invited for a celebration at the mansion of vizier Nasrat al-Din. When he offered me to accompany him, I asked about the people who were also attending. All the elite were supposed to come. I accepted the idea thinking that it was just the occasion I wanted. We went there together and sat in a corner. The chamber was full of *Amir*s, merchants, scholars and Sufis. They started speaking. Each of them began conveying the words of a past scholar and told about the miracles of a saint. I only listened to them silently. Their speech was so arid and artificial that I could not help shouting.

- Until what time will you go on with the words of such people? When will you say, "My heart told it from an inspiration of my Lord? Why do you walk with the staff of others? Where are your own words and works?

All lowered their heads and could not utter a single word. However, I awoke the grudge and envy against myself. If someone who did not understand me saw what I was doing, he would say, "This man is looking for trouble". Everybody was petrified. I said to Mawlana.

- It is not possible to pick flowers in fake springs; the words soften in the mouths of lovers but this place is where words became mud. Let us go. The effect of my severe words could be seen on their blushed faces. We left, without even saying good-bye.

The number of my enemies was increasing each day. I was growing the flames greater. I went to an inn at the bazaar one day. I entered and saw that the locals- rather than the customers – were sitting down and eating like grasshoppers as if they had come out of famine.

Oh people, oh the group of idles! I heard that you are gossiping about me here and there baselessly. You say that Shams does not belong to any sect. You are right. I know all religious sects but I do not follow any of them. I smelled all flowers but did not become a leaf of any flower. I am a man of affection but I do not have a certain way. I speak but I do not write. I read but I am not a slave of books. I read from the hearts, not from leather or pages. You thought that I am a beggar. You may think as you wish. I do not demand money from you. I will be rewarded by Him. Enjoy your *tirit* (a kind of meal made of meat, bread and yoghurt –t.n) and kebabs. I will take your sultan, not your food. Your molded and rusty eyes are not aware of that diamond. Do not tarnish my candle. Open my way and devour your meals. I hate books, women and whims. I came here to feed those who are in need of love. Keep on playing with flesh and bones.

The speech I made in that inn spread through the city. The vultures of gossiping boiled in their pots. Mawlana also heard about what had happened. He came to my room in shyness that evening.

- People of Konya are talking about you, which makes me sad.
- Do not fear, they can give no harm to you and me.
- I wish they admired you as I did.
- I do not need admiration and friendship of others, except from you. You are an ocean and others are a muddy puddle in a pit. My reckless behavior is due to my nature. It is difficult to live with me now. The third wish of Prophet Moses was out of the fire of desire, seeking and divine love, not to meet *Khidr*. The hunger of Moses in this case was not less than that of yours. I have hunger only for you, Mawlana.
- You are right Shams. I am not complaining about the words.
- Now let me tell you a Sufi story, my dear Mawlana. They took a certain Sufi to the physician due to a serious illness. The physician asked, "What's the matter with you? Hearing this question, the sufi startled suddenly and said "I have no complaint". His friends explained the situation to the physician who was surprised. "He is a sufi and never complains. Do not ask what his problem or complaint is. If you want an answer, just ask where the pain is?"

However, we complain about many things; about the smallest things we do not enjoy; from suffering, love, illness, grief and even excessive love and interest. When the wheat is like a fuse, it is not useful; you need to process it at the mill so that you may use it. What can we do with the seeds unless they are sewn under earth? Those complaints may sometimes put us under the ground, but the end is always good; it will blossom like all seeds…

How many sieves of love should I pass through
To drink seven oceans with a single sip?

During early March in 1246, I suddenly disappeared from Konya. No one saw me arriving in Konya in the past and no one should see me leaving now. I came without being invited and I wanted to leave there with no farewell. Leaving Konya was inevitable. It was not a sort of fleeing. I did not offend anyone. Leave those who think that I am going due to fear alone. If I love Mawlana, then I have to leave that place. If you love someone, this means that you only demand goodness for that person. And you should know when to leave for the sake of the friend. Via my mysterious departure, it was necessary to learn if Mawlana was raw or matured. It was a sacrifice; a sacrifice for the friend and a farewell for him. I ought to leave despite my sorrow. This was the right thing for both of us. I had to go into darkness, growing my injuries as abysses. I was not thinking of anyone except Mawlana.

The candles of the sky were luminous, but the ones in the city were dim. The darkness was so intense in Konya streets. There was a dry cold that could freeze the breath and people were in their beds. The candles at the *dargah* were dimmed one by one. There was no light in Mawlana's room. A dervish was waiting at the door. I greeted him and said, "I will go for a walk." I left the city after passing by desolated paths and left the perplexed ones with their cunning minds. I was moving like a ghost under the moonlight, from night to an unknown direction:

"Be like a strange wanderer in the world!"

I was still walking at dusk. I saw a steppe village ahead. I entered into a stable. I made a mattress using the bushes. Then I fell asleep. I was woken up by the voices of villagers. They gave me fresh bread. I did not have a single penny. I asked them if they had any job for me. I was thinking of working for a while to afford buying a donkey. I got a grey donkey in return for working in a villager's field. I rode it towards the lands where the sun rose. I arrived in my homeland, Tabriz.

It was years that I had not seen Tabriz. As a gentle hail was drizzling, I visited the family graveyard with tears in my eyes. I prayed for my dead family members. I did not want to stay there long. My real intention was looking for Mawlana's scent in the cities where he spent his childhood.

The years of grief began. Greif is one of the states of separation. Is not the world a kind of gloomy exile? Grief suits lovers very well. We burnt and were burnt; but never complained about grief. Is not it true that we are the followers of a grieved Prophet? Grief keeps the wounds of love fresh. I enjoy my injuries and my beloved.

If a wave of grief fills one's heart, this means that either he missed his Master or his Master missed him. Trouble, grief and sorrow were the whip Mawlana showed his beloved ones. The more he heats, the more he attracts. Grief is the cloth in which my Lord had woven Mawlana in my heart as longing.

Wherever I looked, I happened to see Mawlana. I saw him if I looked at the sky or into water. Mawlana was in the sound of winds and on the turtledove of my dreams; in the glimmer of stars and in fountains in the mosques. You are in my soul but my soul is unaware of you… the world is full of you and unaware of you… how can my heart find you? For, you are entirely in my heart… but you are unaware of the heart. Oh

Mawlana, my beloved; I concealed my heart in places which nobody knows; my exiled and free heart was with you. You knew not, I grew the orphan in my heart. I had to leave. I quenched my thirst for you only by your absence. The most inaccessible dream was to see you. They thought Shams did not deserve an imagination, not to speak of reality.

I can neither abandon you nor attain you. My eyes close with your longing each night, the morning sun becomes pale by the pain of separation each morning. I had to put an end to my love, which I could not hide, and I had to leave as I arrived.

My tears dropped saying "you" while I was leaving. I am as near as breath although you are far away as distant as life. I will breathe with you in your heart with my scent after I become a flower in spring. I will come and illuminate you with a handful of the sun in my eyes when you hide yourself in your darkness. I do not want to hear anybody… I want only to live and see. You are my only reality that I could not fit in any imagination. I loved as such…

I knew that my loss will hurt Mawlana deeply but sacrifice is another name of love… I learnt afterwards that my friend offended those who caused my separation. He entered his cell and plunged into the fire of separation. This was predestined, this was required for Mawlana to be Mawlana. He took a pen and paper, and inscribed his laments.

He came to Damascus a few times in search of me. These visits were in fact relieves from distress. He knew that he would not find me unless I wished to appear. Mawlana, who came to Damascus like a partridge, returned to Konya like a falcon. Love is to accept loneliness…

There is no solution for the equation of love. One should get used to it. Man can learn to be loved without tasting it. However, he/she must live loving and affliction. Only then, there will be an attachment to life…

I was wondering in the Afghani villages like a lunatic, not in Damascus. I was busy with showing the right path to the perplexed *Rafizi*s in *Hashashi dargah*s of Afghanistan. This way, I believed that I might console the pain of separation from Mawlana. I was in vain. My pain deepened day by day. Therefore, I decided to console my grief by his memories and scent in the streets of Damascus where I saw him first. Thus, I intended to return to Damascus.

I disgraced an admired shaykh called Seyyed Shahmar before his disciples. I told him that he was not a real shaykh and he deceived the public. I could not help speaking again. His dervishes almost killed me there. When the public gathered around me, they stopped. Seyyid Shahmar was shouting behind me:

- What is wrong with you? You were not very normal in the past but you were not mad as such. I think this happened in Konya. By God, I will make Konya your graveyard. Do not forget that you will have troubles worse than Mongolian devils!

Mawlana was busy with looking for me and his grief surrounded Konya. The people there had uneasy days. What if Mawlana does not return to Konya due to his offense for what had happened and settled in Damascus? Then this city would be barren with his absence. This great capital city would be dry and pale without him. People of Konya conveyed their anxiety to the officials of the palace. They wrote letters and requested him to turn back. Our friend Mawlana returned to his home. I arrived in Damascus, to the city of the beloved the following day. Mawlana was looking for me in the city of love, Konya whereas I was in search of his memory in the rooms of inns and in the streets of Damascus.

Mawlana returned to Konya as he lost the hope of finding me in Damascus. He dreamt that I was in an inn in Damascus. He wrote a letter in the morning and sent it with a dervish. He told the dervish:

- If you return with good news, ask from me whatever you wish.
- I wish the health of your heart.
- Go with divine peace and return with good news.

I told the innkeeper in Damascus the fact and threatened him:

- You do not know me. If he asks any question, just tell him that I have not come here for months. If you do not do what I said, I will make your inn collapse with my curse.

The dervish brought the letter but was disappointed by the innkeeper's words. He trusted the letter to the innkeeper having a little hope of my visit there.

"I asked about you not to those who seek peace, nor found it, nor those who escape from peace. Who can tell the heat of the sun best? One who faints by the heat? No, his love is weak. How about one who travels to the sun? No, where can he reach at last? One should not ask about the sun to whom takes shelter in shadow…

The sanctuary of love… My master… can you tell me what is the meaning of all these suffering? If the mystery of this separation is to harden the flames you cast on my heart, did not I melt in the pots of fire sufficiently? I burnt so much that;

Let me burn as you burn!

Let me freeze as you freeze!

"Will you make me long for you by fleeing towards the Milky Way again?.. My longings disperse everywhere like the dry dianthus those thrown into empties in the breast of pain…The sun has not risen since you left… However, I wanted to go up to sky with you… My hair turned white due

to the burden of this love… all the doors where I I supplicate to firmament and demand mercy is closed. The pulpit and the niche of my life that float in the gray floods are in you… the call for funeral is recited for me now… my tears fall on to my praying mat each dawn, but your voice and breath come from far away…

The calls for prayer are recited day by day lamenting. But a purl hurts my temples which will not attain peace unless I touch my forehead on yours… it is as if there are horsemen from Daghistan on my forehead… and my hands sometimes tremble… This is the intense scent of madness… my shoulders are lowered as I think of you… Do not forget that I who am your work transformed into ruins day by day… But you still are not turning to me!.. My wish is that may the Lord of the Universe does not let the value and importance of this love be evaluated by anyone else…"

"My thought disperses as the rosary beads with your absence…I want to make pearls out of my tears for you now… I wish you were here… my words become like a waterfall whenever I attempt to write anything concerning you… you never know how my burning forehead is in need of your merciful hands… none of our memories may be forgotten although you put me into fire… I will reborn like Phoenix out of my ashes and continue to my way fluttering like the groups of cranes…

"A drowsiness remained in my eyes from the sleeping with your absence… A trouble on my chest that I could not swallow… My breaths do not suffice for this poor soul…I fixed my eyes on the ceiling and thought only of you… I have drops of cold sweat on my forehead… my ears cannot hear anything other than your voice in this world… My eyelids are wide open lest your image might be veiled… I have no salt of yearning in my tears that would console my pain…

My blood is freezing… a sort of coldness penetrates into my soul suddenly… I do not have your warmth with me… then it is morning again, I am depressed with a thousand of troubles and grief! I am grieved out of that separation… you know, you are my sultan… my beloved and sanctuary… you are what I seek; the exalted one of seven heavens; free us from this yearning…"

The butterflies spread their wings into the gardens on which your face touched. I am trying to come out of this narrow cocoon of my chest. The secret of vast broadness is hidden between your lips. Say something! I want to hear the tune of each syllable. Let the winds blow me, your rains drop on my forehead and let all stones fall on my chest. Let me be an enormous mountain that kisses your feet. Let the deserts be scattered and mountains be removed between us. Let the ascents and descents finish so that I may be dust on the path you walk. I am in a desert and thirsty. I am Joseph in the wells. Your words are like Zulaiha for me. I am Ibrahim in the fire. Your eyes are oceans for me. I am Mary in pain. Your sight is like Jesus for me. I am Job in injuries. Your longing is healing for me. I am a dead among dead bodies. Your hands are musalla (a huge stone where coffins are put before funeral prayer – t.n) for me.

Oh, the light in our hearts! Come the end of my mourning and desires. You know that my life is in your hands. Do not make the life and your servants troubled, come! Oh lover! Oh the beloved! Pass over the obstacles and leave persistence. Oh the owner of hoopoes, Solomon! Show us mercy and come here to look for us.

The souls are lamenting due to your loss; complete your task and come forth. Conceal the bad sides and open the goodness. This is the habit of generous ones, come forth. How do you say, "come" in Persian? "Biya"? Either come or accept our invitation and come forth. When you come, our luck will be opened. If you do not come, it will be dead; come oh Qushad of Arabs! Oh Qubad of Persia! Come and conquer my heart with your money. I invite you sincerely. Oh the being that will exist within itself, come.

You went. It would be pleasant if you stayed. You went but everything concerning you is in me. I have your absence in me. You went: woe on me! My gentle heart became a moth in your absence.

Not all lonely people are lovers; but all burnt ones are alone in the shadow of love. I say I burnt out of your fireless, not of your fire. Oh the voice of love, come soon and let the noise of apocalypse be consoled…

After reading the letter, I smelled it and put it on my chest. I did not write a reply. I received another letter the following month. The second one was longer but more pleasant!

"Oh the most elegant one in the world! Peace be upon you. My illness and health are in your hands. Tell your slave what the remedy for his illness is. If I receive a kiss, it is that which I receive from your lips. If I cannot reach your service by my body, my soul and heart are with you. Now that speaking exists via words, then why did this world fill with "I am in your service"?

Oh my heart, pain, love, grief, suffering! Oh my livable in silence and my flame in speaking. Oh my grief that comes down like the scattered pearls, oh whom disperses on the necks of noble bridesmaid. Oh my migration that set off on the way I found without searching. You are the one I could not attain and could not satisfy even in attainment. Oh whom I cannot stay out and cannot come out; the owner of nights and the spring of my tears; I could not remove your dust and clean your rust. Oh my darkness and sun! Oh my heart and exalted friend! Where art thou, return to your home or write to us… who made your archly heart offended? Which evil word and insidious sight tore you from me, oh Shams? You are all that I have. Don't you know that I am nothing if you do not exist? Do not give Mawlana, who is drunk for your worlds, your separation as a gift. Do not, oh Shams!

I heard that you attempt to leave us, don't
You incline to another friend, don't
What do you do, oh stranger, in a foreign realm
Which ill hearted you me, don't
Do not take us from ourselves and do not go to those realms,
You cast your sight over those stolen ones, don't
The skies are ruined for you, oh the moon
Just as you ruined us, don't

Oh you whose station is above the existent and the nonexistent
You leave the field of being, don't
If you turn your face, the moon becomes darkened out of your grief,
And you attempt to collapse the house of the moon, don't
Our lips become dry if you become dry,
You make our eyes burst into tears, don't
If you do not have enough strength to overwhelm lovers
Then why are you surprised for love, don't
Oh you in whose hands are the hell and paradise
You make paradise a hell for us, don't
The poison in sugar bowl does not harm us,
You make that sugar as poison, don't...
You make us joyful, but we may lose peace,
You make my peace ruined, don't
My eyes that fell into unlawful is the thief of your beauty
Oh you who touch even theft; you steal, don't
It is not the time to speak of friend, rebel
Why are you dealing with the drunkenness of love, don't.

I was looking for profundity in the books before you. I feel shame for the books. You are more profound than the books; I am ashamed of the books I wrote to you; read yourself.

I was in darkness and the sound of madness whips on my face: laughter of owls, a whistle of a cobra… I am in darkness. The only source of light that illuminated my dungeon was your singing. Oh my star, you are now far away. Oh Shams, you are pure as a sincere tear and illuminated as sight of a child; what is it to the source if the jackals in a desert drank water.

I am so full of you that even my skull would be crashed. You were the blood flowing in my veins. The heart in my chest was your heart. It was as if my chest would split and my veins would crack. I was breathing you. The wings of separation brought me down from the sky. But we were flying with you there.

I lived each night with fever because of your absence. Perhaps fever was even better. However, to what extent can an organism endurer this tension? I owe too much for love. I want to be melted in that fever; to burn in that fire and turn into ash is what I sought: to be ash, light and a legend.

I am you and you are me. We experience the same scents, same excitements and pains. One can enter paradise through purgatory. Mary of Magdalena washed Jesus' injured feet with her tears and dried them with her hair. I wish you came and I could wash your feet those were weary of bushes on the roads and were afflicted by the weariness of years, oh my Crown…

Oh Shams! Even Salah al-Din Zarqub's tears cannot extinguish the fire of yearning inside me. You are the only remedy; I wish you came…

I wish I would set off, cry, pray and crash on the ways just like the Sidra of heavens, find remedies on the peaks and swallow abysses only for you. I would tell the pain in my heart part by part and cry to the extent of splitting. I would say that my pride became the place of halwah and I have no words to utter. I would say that the sprinkles fall with hope in my ears those became naked on your way. Won't you come, oh Shams, after all these?

I do not know where I am in this journey. I sometimes stand and then fall immediately. I sleep with dead poems and feel coldness. I wonder if this blind well has an end.

Oh Shams, which word made your gentle heart offended, and which evil eye injured your dark sight that you left for unknown realms? Don't you know that your friend is wondering in madness after your leaving? Come, oh Shams, for the sake of Moses who fainted on Sinai, for the sake of Jesus who cried in Jerusalem and for the sake of Mohammad Muhtar who cried saying "my ummah" in Medina. Konya does not smell like love any longer.

"Your Mawlana"

I read the letter and looked up to the sky through my window. A stone fell down the sky and a tear dropped unto my chest. I was murmuring the following words while I was thinking of Mawlana by the window! Each word of yours is a kiss, did you write them by your lips, oh holy man? They were like fire; did you split your heart and rub the envelope with it? I take the worlds in my hands and caress them. Some of them are as hard as diamond, they make my hands bleed; some of them are as soft as velvet and warm as tears. I sanctify all my pains. I do not have any intention of writing. There is no answer for the patient better than patience.

The third letter came several weeks later:

"If the roses do not bloom as Shams, what should I do with the scent of roses? What should I do with the darkness of nights if they do not make the separation weep? What should I do with honey and burgers without Shams? What should I do with the pain if it does not burn me? What should I do with tears if they do not burn my eyes? What should I do with the beloved if it is not Shams for my darkness; what should I do with the friend that does not sacrifice his soul on my path? What should I do with the eyes that do not look like Shams? What should I do with the words that do not serve as remedy for the beloved's heart? Give the final decree of Heavens! Why do you rotate in the universe if Shams is not here? What should I do with Adam that does not live the universe in a single atom and love in the whole universe?

To get used to your absence... all words of consolation is like betrayal in my ears. It is quite strange that the ones who were criticizing you in the past were talking to console Mawlana who is in the yearning of your absence. My fingers are burning in flames. I fear that the paper will flame up and letter will burn. To be far from you in order to gain you is worse than hell.

You were the one whom I have waited for forty years. You were to one whom I found late. Now that you are not here, for how long should I wait? I am as thirsty as the sand in deserts. May your approaching be the spring rain. Do you remember that you put a huge copper pot in the courtyard of our dargah so that it should be filled with the April rains and we may break our fast with blissful rainwater? Won't you blossom oh my rose of heart that soaked with April rains?

Your words are still new in my ears. Your letters are like stars. Your sentences are the greatest moonlight. I remember your smile. Your sunlight smile is a pleasant morning as good as attainment. We are the soul that broadens, unites and eternalizes with each other.

Come, oh Shams, may your feet be qudum (a kind of drum used during Mawlawi rites –t.n), your arms be rabab and come as your breath blows the good news of attainment. You are a fountain, the more I drink the more I become thirsty. You are a fire in which I become cooler the more I burnt. You are apparently consisting of flesh and bones; but you carry in your heart the entire humanity.

What if I see hundred worlds without seeing your face?

To whom should I ask about your beauty; suppose that I ask it for everyone, who may tell about it? What if I stay in paradise forever, the houris are my wives and I have a good heart unless I attain you?

What should I do with the cloud that rained pearls and germs on my head if that cloud of separation veiled your moonlike face?

Now that this world which is like a wicked magician will extinct one day, what should I do with the ranks, fate and the treasures of it if they give them to me?

I don't care if the entire world revile against me due to your love. Even if hundreds of lies are ascribed about the truth, who cares?

Love was my silence! Love was my fire! Love was my rapture and my fire! Love was my restriction and confession! Love was my excitement! It was my only being and extinction… my injury and remedy…it was the one that I could not gain but lost each time. Right, love was as such! I missed, oh Shams. Come forth for the sake of Allah!

I learnt that love grows and ripens man. No one has taught me that love is unanswered. I did not know that only the one who loves sincerely will burn with this pain and the one who is loved cannot know he/she is loved… glories be to "You"! You let me feel the things that are not taught in life. You made me feel what I did not make anyone feel. I made what I could not for anyone. Am I regretful? No, I never regret. I am happy even when hiding love in my eternity. You made me enjoy love in the last days of my life. Thank you for allowing me to love you."

This last letter burnt my heart. I hesitated whether to write a reply or not. On the one hand, the fire of longing and on the other hand the sacrifice for Mawlana; for love and for the sake of love. I had to go for the sake of love. I never liked writing since my childhood. I would return on one condition. Would he be able to write the word that would let me set off? I wrote a reply to find out.

"If you are a man of love, do not be ignorant or complain. You say you missed me in your letters. Did your burnt heart write only a dry "I missed you"? Understand Mawlana. Cry Mawlana. This separation was a lesson for whom can understand it. This grief was the cause of your crying. Do not be ignorant, a familiar one will come and remove your tears. Do not cry, my dear Mawlana.

It was necessary to experience the unanswered love. I did not know that it was during autumn one loves the other and experiences the beauty of affliction by a madly love. I learnt that I missed many things in life… either I came here early or you are so late for attainment…

Do not expect a strange laugh from me. I am happy with my pains. Happiness is serious and scowling. Both of us were exposed to a storm and we do not know where it will throw us. Our separation is either as long as centuries or as short as a dream. To transform centuries into attainment is depended to a single word of yours…

Write to me such a word that I may flee from Damascus and fly to Konya for it. Write down a word and make me scattered, make me a moth… a word that is not enlisted in dictionaries; a word that is not told by anyone to anybody, one that may extinguish the hell… write it down so that Shams may come there and be the dust under your feet."

They told me that when he received the letter Mawlana's joy was like that of children during religious festivals. My words flew up to the sky, to the heart of the beloved. My words became music for Mawlana. Now all the scents are frail, all the poems are pale and all songs are tuneless for Mawlana. He climbed up the heaves as he read my letter, at the peaks where great sufferers and saints, where great souls fly. He repeatedly smelled and read my letter saying " I feel shame for myself; I am earth and you are Heaven. I am skin and you are the heart. I am the flame and you are the light." Then he put the letter inside his shirt and sighed deeply. He took the letter out as passing the *Sidrat al-Muntaha* and read it again losing his consciousness. He fainted there in joy… He woke up in another dream. When he touched the paper on his chest, he realized that it was transformed into a white rose. He smelled the rose and began crying. He tore a leaf slowly; then touched his fingertip on his tears and moistened it. Then touched the leaf and wrote a single word on a piece of paper: "*Hamush*" (i.e. the silent one; the cemeteries are called *Hamushan*, that is the 'the silent ones' – t.n).

I opened the envelope that innkeeper brought and then read it immediately. The word I wished to return was there, there was no sense to stay there. I could not bear my *Hamush* to be clay again among the raw ones. I had to return in any case; either the Hamush would be "love" or I would die for the sake of love.

I hope complaining this much for the beloved is forgiven for a lover. Yes, I lived, I saw and I learnt. Love can be realized only by one person. It is unanswered. Some people know only to love, but they love without thinking whether the other person loves or not. He/ she waits to be loved and sees at last that the other one tries to give a reply forcing himself/herself not to offend you. There is no offence in love. If you love, if you feel love really in your heart, you have to set the beloved free so that he/she may live wherever he/she is happy… It is necessary to learn observing his happiness affair and heal his injuries…

My aim was to remember your name in the beats of your heart. What I demanded was not to make you weep. However, you were casting a tear by each letter and trembling as the sun rotated inside you. Oh, love! It was you who burnt in flames; but why is it that my left side is cold?

What a spring you are, oh Mawlana?
The thirstier I became the more I drink you.

I wrote to Mawlana that I was tired but would endure the journey. I told him that he had better send Sultan Walad to Damascus for the fear that I might quit returning after questioning whether my return is good or bad for me.

Mawlana called Sultan Walad as soon as he received my letter:

- Go to Damascus at once and bring our master here.

Sultan Walad set off for Damascus together with gifts and about twenty dervishes. Sultan Walad, who loved me as much as his father did, journeyed without resting. The twenty dervishes also exerted their utmost efforts to arrive in Damascus as soon as possible and bring me back to Konya. They never stopped on the way, they passed mountains and plains day and night.

Finally, the delegation of the friend saw Damascus ahead. In the meantime, I was staying at *Jabal al-Salahiyya* Inn. I was playing chess with a young Christian in my room. My door was knocked three times. Sultan Walad and a few young dervishes entered in silently. They were as tender as a dear that was entrapped by a hunter. There were no words or greetings. Time also remained still. They were as if shadows flew through the window. They were waiting for my reaction. I behaved as if they were not there. Sultan Walad took my slippers on the rug. He turned its direction towards Konya. His excited heart made his hands tremble. I looked into his eyes; they were ready to burst into tears at any moment. The other dervishes filled my shoes with gold coins from his moneybag. I stood up from the sofa. Their faces were lowered and they turned their backs to the door. They did not turn their backs towards me out of respect…

I threw the coins out of the window. The public gathered around the gate of the inn. I gave all the gifts Mawlana sent me to the poor. I opened my arms and embraced my spiritual sons for minutes. Sultan Walad was crying and I was crying, too. I turned to him and said:

- Is there any gift more valuable than Mawlana for me? My Lord let me meet him as a reward of enduring the trouble of years. He is a great bliss for one who knows. Both the dervishes inside the room and the ones waiting outside kissed my hands:

- Forgive us, oh Shaykh. However much tears we shed from the eyes that do not see your spiritual rank are in vain. The dervishes not only kissed my hands continuously but also beat their chests. At the same time, the people of Damascus were trying to understand what was happening:

- Let us make our way; we should not let the beloved wait longer.

- I thought about what had been experienced following my unexpected departure. Sultan Walad was telling me what had happened when we rested on the way to return. The dervishes residing at the *dargah* woke up by a noise more severe than thunder. When they came into the courtyard, Mawlana was shouting and crying. "Where is my Shams, where is he, what did you do to him?" He was tearing his garments and throwing the stones everywhere. He had no shoes and his *dastagul* (a kind of shirt worn by Mawlawis – t.n) was torn; he knelt down on the stone ground and went on shouting half conscious: "You stone –hearted ones! You wicked ones! Finally, you reached what you desired. I lost my beloved. How should I live now and then?" Sultan Walad cried together with his father. As the crowd in the courtyard grew bigger, Sultan Walad brought his father to his room; he cleaned his father's tears and said "Do not weep and make yourself grieved, oh father, I will find your friend for you". Mawlana who went to his room with difficulty slept there the whole day. He hardly ever left his room except for Friday prayers. He almost gave up eating and drinking due to grief. He tried to find consolation with the nay player, the conversations with Salah al-Din Zarqubî. By the way, we'd better tell something concerning Salah al-Din Zarqubî:

Salah al-Din Faridun was born in a village of Konya. He came to Konya and learnt goldsmithery there. He opened a shop and earned his living. As a pious and virtuous person, Salah al-Din was initiated by Mawlana's father's friend and *muqaddam* (one who represents a shaykh t.n) *Seyyid Burhan al-Din.* He advanced on Sufi path by his supreme morality and piety. He got permission (*ijaza*) from *Seyyed Burhan al-Din* and became a sheikh. His shaykh admired this pure love of God too much. In fact, Salah al-Din was illiterate: but he was pious and an illuminated believer who feared Allah. He was full of Divine love and gained many spiritual states. Salah al-Din Zarqubi (Salah al-Din the Jeweller) returned to his village after his Shaykh Seyyed Burhan al-Din went to Kayseri. He got married there and had many children.

He returned to Konya on a Friday night. He entered the Abu'l Fadl Mosque in order to pray. After the prayer, Mawlana began preaching. He was admonishing them excitedly and eloquently. During his sermon, Mawlana was talking about virtues, love and spiritual states of his Shaykh Burhan al-Din. As Salah al-Din the jeweler was listening to Mawlana by heart, he saw Seyyed Burhan al-Din in Mawlana's personality as a great light. It was as if Mawlana went away and Seyyed

Burhan al-Din came and sat there saying beautiful words instead. When Seyyed Burhan al-Din gained his conscious again, he stood up and began shouting as a madman. He ran towards Mawlana. When he came under the pulpit where Mawlana was preaching, he bowed down before him. These are what dervishes told me.

Salah al-Din Zarqubi admired Mawlana so much and had great respect for him. Both of them had the spiritual blessings of the same Shaykh, Burhan al-Din Tirmidhi. Mawlana also loved Shaykh Salah al-Din and never ceased helping him. But following my arrival, Mawlana saw nobody except for me thus Salah al-Din became looked at me with hostile eyes. I was unknown also for him.

Mawlana told his admirers: "Do not mention Shams in the presence of Salah al-Din and about Salah al-Din in the presence of Husam al-Din. There is no distinction between them, but this would be better from the point of morality. The spiritual men have a divine jealousy." Salah al-Din also had a deep loyalty for Mawlana. One day Mawlana said, "I didn't know that I had the sources of light inside of me. You discovered me and made me ecstatic."

After my sudden departure from Konya, Mawlana became distressed and he was seeking consolation by wondering and talking with Salah al-Din. He left his *dargah* only to pray Friday prayer in Iplikci Mosque. One day, he heard the harmonious sound of his hammer while passing by Salah al-Din's jewelry store. Then he felt ecstasy with this sound, began whirling, and Salah al-Din went on hammering the gold without thinking that he would waste it under the hammer. When Salah al-Din went out of the shop, he saw Mawlana's joyful state and said:

- Praise be to Allah, our Pîr regained his happy state as in the past. Oh friends, I may sacrifice all my shops and goods in this bazaar. Take whatever you want. Then he participated in *sama*. After they finished whirling, his neighbors said:

- What did you do, oh Salah al-Din? People despoiled the goods in your shop. You lost almost everything.

- Let the possessions be the property of the slaves of the world. Our eyes saw Mawlana in happiness. Then let all my property be like a tip for his good news.

People of Konya were envious also against Mawlana's love and respect for Salah al-Din the jeweler. Those who are deprived of divine love, who could not overwhelm their desires and ambitions via praying and self- denial, were jealous of Salah al-Din the jeweler as they were once against me. They said:

- We got rid of one (that is Shams) and now have even a worse one. The former was light but this is sparkle. Shams' words were reasonable and the way he spoke was good. He was a virtuous and wise man. He let us write meaningful worlds. He wishes to remain as a friend of Mawlana here.

Mawlana enjoyed being relatives with his friends in order to strengthen the ties of love. He let his daughter Fatima Hatun marry Sultan Walad.

Sultan Walad went on telling the effects of my sudden departure. I felt an unexplainable feeling as I listened to him.

Those who felt sad as much as Mawlana after my departure were not more than a few people; Salah al-Din, Husam al-Din, Atashbaz, Sultan Walad and Kimya Hatun whom I never saw but who observed me from far away.

Young dervishes, the imams of the mosques, shaykhs of Konya and the exoteric *molla*s who feared love had a deep joy with my departure. It was strange that there were both a joy of festivals and a state of mourning in Konya. I was amazed at the degree of my influence.

- I do not care about the public. Go on telling me about the *dargah*, oh SultanWalad.

- After your mysterious departure, he became like an ecstatic that abandoned all worldly things. He was either looking for you in the streets from morning to evening or wondering at night with torn clothes for the hope of your coming to the courtyard. The disciples feared meeting him because of their penitence. They were blaming each other "It is we that caused this state by offending Shams."

After losing the hope for your coming, my father stopped going out. He closed his door to the public and isolated himself from everything. He whirled on stones until they became blooded and prayed until he fell down from weakness. During some nights, he was shouting, "I wish I could run away from this house like Shams". I stopped him.

- That will do, Sultan Walad. I walked away from the camp place. I took some soil from the ground and cried, "Tell me, oh earth, did Mawlana walk here?"

Konya was anxious. The night was covering the streets with its painful wings. The public had uneasiness… There was certain regret in the houses. Mawlana was protesting in hunger. He began fasting his fast of attainment (*wisal*) but this time an *iftar* for seven days of fasting instead of once in three days. His body was tired and he was sick. He accepted the examination of the doctor with Sultan Walad's insistence. He could not eat whatever Atashbaz cooked for them. He only wanted to die and put an end to his depression with the breath of death. Salah al-Din wanted to speak through the window and Husam al-Din spoke behind the door, but he was in vain. He did not want to talk to anyone. He only ate a few slices of bread and a little yoghurt by the efforts of Sultan Walad himself.

The people realized that his condition was getting worse, they said "We have to find or let somebody find Shams for our Master" and they decided to talk with Mawlana via Husam al-Din. All those people who were against me and blamed me for heresy came to Mawlana altogether and said, "We could not understand Mawlana. Forgive us. We will exert our utmost efforts to let you meet again. Please, come out. Just show yourself in the bazaar. Forgive us, oh Mawlana". These excuses and sincerity helped a little, and Mawlana began writing the letters.

As Sultan Walad knew that the only hope that keeps Mawlana conscious was depending on my returning from Damascus, he continuously sent news such as "we almost found Shams; we are on the way" to keep him energetic.

Finally, I saw the spring on the steppe, the snow-white light of Konya plains.

I was alone wherever I went. I had no shadows. I was not sleeping at nights and closed for the crowded streets during the day. I either sat down and invoked in my wicked room or contemplated under a tree until the dusk when people went to their houses and the streets were emptied. I was alone to the extent that I could not think about the old days. The pain hardens the sensitiveness and then turns into a sort of habit. To remain in the middle of pain is sweeter than sweet dreams. I began living not by burning but by being burnt or at least smoking. I am a sixty-eight- year old plane tree, my roots overspread the deserts; my trunk threw out its cover; one end of my branches reaches Konya and the other end goes to Damascus. The silence I grew inside me for years is becoming an abyss.

I do not pay any attention to whatever they think of me. The people of my era could not understand me, nor did the writers. I did not run away from Konya. I am not capricious and I did not offend anyone.

There were ones who had an enmity against me. There were ones who cursed me and they provoked the young dervishes called "*Fatayan*" against me. The youngsters are energetic. They are excited and move by mottos. As these young dervishes went on growing enmity against me, they were deprived of courage. They were afraid of my sight. They were full of enmity during the day but they calmed down during the night.

We were going along Tigris. I told the caravan:

- Let us stop for a while… Let us hear the sound of flowing water. Let us run under the sky and embrace a tree; and pray there together for the forgiveness of our faults. Let us cry for love and water the earth with our tears.

I loaded my bag onto the back of the horse. I bent down and took grabbed soil. I smelled it… I started the longest journey inwardly… the earth was barren… a mountain afar, its peak was covered with snow…

I remembered my youth… The only living thing with me was my donkey. And the coffin next to an oak tree. I used to sleep in that coffin as silent as death. I felt the magnificent harmony of the invoking of my nature and of the universe in my dreams. When I woke up, I thought that the dream seen in a single moment was perhaps an entire life…

- Master, is everything all right with you? If you like, we may stop here to rest.

I raised my head by the voice of sultan Walad; I came nearer to him and held his right hand:

- Son! Bring your fingers and put them on my left side. Silence… Silence…

- Silence is the best rest. I am tired of words. If the words do not come out of the mouth after becoming breath, you become silent. In order to return to the lived moment, you wait for a single word in a nature that has no confines. Finally, a word that understands you approaches. By that single word, the Supreme Name, you heart begins beating. The letters of the alphabet, the breath of human. Thus, one breathes when he/she recites the Holy Quran. How about reciting Quran under that tree?
- All right master.

I lowered my head silently and embraced the tree. I started crying. Then I had *wudu* with the cold water of the river. My tearful condition was going on. My tears mixed with the water of the river. I was not certain whether my tears moistened the river or it was the river that moistened me. I said sobbing, "Oh my Mawlana".

We were having long talks with Sultan Walad on the way either riding on the horses or as we stopped to pray in a garden. I arrived in Aleppo. Everywhere was completely green. The gardens were in joy of spring. I wished to attain my dear Mawlana as soon as possible. We had ablution and prayed our canonical prayer.

I wanted Sultan Walad to be the Imam.

- Oh Master, if I be the imam before you, I will faint.
- You are Mawlana's son. It is about time you became the imam. Now let me recite the call for prayer.

After the prayer, I told them that I wanted to be alone and went for a walk in the garden. I wandered the whole day in the fields. It was getting dark. As the sun was dragging its light from the garden and the moon was spreading its plumage light on the flowers, as I was sitting under the trees and watching the stars that shone as silver flakes on a blue carpet among the bushes, I realized how unusual the sky was.

In the meantime, I was listening to the happy growling of a small river.

I lost myself as I was watching the sleeping nature under that tree. I saw a dead bird in a cage in my dream. I saw that the cage transformed into a human skeleton suddenly and the dead bird into a human heart that bleeds due to a deep wound like the lips of a sorrowful woman. The wound said, "I am the heart of a human being, captive of matter and victim of worldly rules."

"I was imprisoned in a cage made of rules which were made by man by the river of life and in the field of beauty. I died in the middle of beatific creation. I was prevented from enjoying Allah's generosity and freedom. Everything in the name of beauty that evokes love and passion inside me according to human understanding is disgrace; and each beautiful thing that I see according to his judgment is in vain." I am a heart of a lost person imprisoned in a wicked prison of human orders; a dead heart forgotten by man who entertains himself, chained by worldly authority, speeches and whose eyes are devoid of tears. I woke up by SultanWalad's words,

- Master, it is time to go and it is getting colder. I do not want you get cold.
- You are right son, we'd better get ready. Why did not you warn me before?
- You were sleeping so sweet that I did not want to disturb you. Moreover, I feared the shadows of light over your head.
- Do not tell what you saw to anybody else.
- All right, master.
- Son, you know humanity is busy with all worldly matters, but I have always tried to hold a flambeau of love so that it may purify me and remove mercilessness from my heart.

- I filled my hands with fog once. Then I opened my hands but the fog became an earthworm. I closed and reopened them; there was a human being in grief. Then I closed and opened them but this time, there was only fog in them.

- Oh Pir, I wonder something concerning your sudden departure from Konya; which one is easier, to stay or to leave?

- Konya says, "Do not leave me, for, your past resides here" and the road says "come and follow me, for, I am your future… I say to the both, "I have neither past nor future. If I stay here, my stay has a departure and my departure has a stay. Only love and death will change everything."

We are on the way. There it is, Mount Erciyes whose peak is covered with snow. We finished most of the way. We are happy that we are so near to Konya. We went to an inn in Konya and had a bath. We were going to the mosque to perform our prayers. I said to the dervishes,

- We will pray not in the mosque but at the station of Seyyed Burhan al-Din, the teacher of my *Hamush*.

- My father will be happy when he hears that we visited the tomb of his teacher and prayed there.

- The reason I liked Seyyed Burhan al-Din is that his honorable posture against the sultans rather than the fact that he was your father's teacher. On the other hand, he educated your father very well.

- I did not know it. Should a shaykh keep away from the sultans?

- A shaykh should never be the guest of a sultan. Even if he visits a sultan, it is the sultan who is the guest. The shaykh goes there only to educate the sultan and teaches him things that will profit him in both worlds, not to take anything from him. A shaykh also should protect himself from the enticement of fame and power. Let me tell you a real story concerning this subject:

A certain sultan visited the *dargah*. He enjoyed the life and the condition of the dervishes there. After paying a few visits, the sultan said to the sheikh,

- I am happy with visiting you and the dervishes. I want to support you in any means. Please allow me to do anything you want.

The Shaykh said,

- Yes, my dear sultan! The only thing I demand is not to visit us here again.

The sultan was shocked:

- Did I commit any fault? I do not know the subtleties of Sufism and I am sorry if I somehow offended you; forgive me.

- No, never sir. You have not offended us. It is my dervishes, not you who caused this. They were invoking the beautiful names of Allah only for His sake before you came. Now they think of you during the *dhikr* and sermons. No, my dear sultan. It is not you; it is we that caused this. I am afraid we do not possess the spiritual maturity to bear your existence here. As a matter of fact that, I have to demand not to visit us again.

We came to Seyyed Burhan al-Din's tomb. We prayed here. I told them to leave me alone there. I wished I could talk to this lover of Allah who tried to educated Jalal al-Din in religious sciences. It was narrated that Burhan al-Din, who was in Horasan when Mawlana's father Baha al-Din Walad died, stood up suddenly and shouted during a scientific meeting:

"Woe on me, my shaykh migrated to the beautiful realm from the street of the realm of earth." Seyyed Burhan al-Din decided to migrate Anatolia expressing that he had to show loyalty as a spiritual guide to Mawlana who was his shaykh's relic.

Seyyed Burhan al-Din tested Mawlana from the point of many sciences and realized that he was trained in the verbal (*qaal*) knowledge. He said to Mawlana, "You went beyond your father a hundred ranks from the point of Ilm al-Yaqin; however, your father was perfect both in verbal knowledge and the knowledge of state (*hal*). I want you to be perfect in *Haqqa'l Yaqin* and *Ayna'l Yaqin* just as your perfectness in *ilm al- yaqin*... I want you to start these levels only by the sufi way and then you may obtain the meaning from me which I gained from my shaykh." Thus, Burhan al-Din implied Mawlana to be his teacher. Mawlana accepted his offer and became a disciple of Burhan al-Din.

Shaykh Burhan al-Din encouraged Mawlana to fight with his self through self-denial. He submitted himself as he submitted his essence in order to get rid of the narrowness of being, of the rust which is the source of grief and sorrow and to open the wings of his own self from the heavens which is the river of joy; and also the world of happiness and to attain the eternal bliss. Shaykh Burhan al-Din was Mawlana's shaykh during his period of rawness. Mawlana was covered entirely with light by the guidance of Burhan al-Din who was a perfect sage.

After staying for a long period in Konya, Seyyed Burhan al-Din decided to return Kayseri. He told Mawlana about this decision a few times. Mawlana said:

"I cannot enjoy this life without you. If my shaykh leaves, my entire life would be nonsense..."

Although Seyyed Burhan al-Din expressed the same idea for a few times, Mawlana prevented him to return to Kayseri by some words similar to the aforementioned ones.

Finally, the desire to return to Kayseri became a yearning for Seyyed Burhan al-Din and one day he set off for Kayseri without informing anyone when he was in sightseeing with his friends.

Although his donkey was normally docile, it suddenly became grumpy when he was directed towards Kayseri and it threw Seyyed Burhan al-Din off his back . Seyyed Burhan al-Din's toes were broken and his leg was injured. His friends came there and caught the animal; they helped him to get on it again. Seyyed Burhan al-Din insisted not to mount the horse; yet the ones who didnt not know what was happening let him forcefully sit on the horse. The animal that threw Seyyed Burhan al-Din off his back suddenly became calm as he turned towards Konya. His friends took him to the village house of a friend. They healed his leg and returned toKonya.

When Seyyed Burhan al-Din came to Mawlana, he reproached Mawlana and said,

- Well done! A disciple breaks his shaykh's leg.

Mawlana felt sorry about what Seyyed Burhan al-Din experienced. He put his hand on his broken fingers, prayed and Seyyed Burhan al-Din's pains calmed down. He felt well soon. Then he allowed him to go to Kayseri.

Thus, Seyyed Burhan al-Din took some food and his donkey; he said his farewells; and left for Kayseri.

Now I am near the tomb of the beautiful person who prepared Mawlana for my coming. I greeted him by prayers and took some soil from his grave, smelled and kissed it.

- Oh, the lover Seyyed! I am in love with the one whom used to be your student once; I am captive of his love. I told him that he trained Mawlana in the best manner and then I left the place. We set off again with Sultan Walad.

People do not seek the beloved; they look for a slave for their egoist feelings. They find a slave, but not the love.

The caravan stopped in a vineyard in Nevsehir to rest. Sultan Walad went on asking interesting questions curiously to to enhance his knowledge through me as usual.

- Oh, master! what can you say on Sufism?
- Sufism is the sect of love. It is to be poor before Allah. To be poor and weak before Him means to accept our dependence to him. The more sincere this acceptance, the stronger it becomes into a motive for the attainment of beloved.
- Who is a shaykh and who is a dervish?
- The relation between the shaykh and his dervish is like the one between a bunch of grapes and the branch on which it is picked from. Shaykh combines grapes to the vine tree, trunk and the roots. The eyes are the mirror of the soul. Shaykhs can read into the disciples by looking in their eyes. The sight of a shaykh is extiemely strong. Every person who wears a cloak or unusual things is not merely a shaykh. However, what is required to be done when you find a shaykh is to submit yourself to him in accordance with what Allah wishes. Call the dervishes here and let me tell you a story:

A shaykh went out to the courtyard to have ablution before *asr* prayer and wanted an ewer from a dervish. The dervish brought it. He knelt down and began ablution while he was busy with looking at the dervishes in the courtyard. The dervish who was pouring water realized that some parts of his hand were dry although he had washed it. The dervish thought:

- Look at him, he thinks that he is a sheikh but he cannot do his ablution properly. He was looking at the shaykh ridiculously. The sheikh raised his head and caught the sight of the dervish. He read what went through the dervishes mind.
- Son, you are not appropriate for us, leave our *dargah* before evening.

The dervish was regretful for his evil thoughts, yet it was too late and he was expelled. He made his farewells to his friends in the evening and left his *dargah* that was situated on the skirts of a desolated mountain. However, he did not know where to go. He had no family and home. He walked day and night unconsciously. He was tired and hungry. It was almost dark. As he was thinking what to do and where to go, he saw a light. He walked to the direction of the light. A shepherd was cooking something under the trees.

- Peace be upon you.
- Peace be upon us.
- Do you have anything to eat for the guest of God?
- Of course, I have. Come and sit here.

The shepherd cast a fast glance over the stranger. Why was this man walking alone in the forest at night? He was not a merchant or a soldier. He had dervish garments on him. Then why was this dervish wandering here at that moment? For, dervishes do not go out in the evenings.

When the dervish told about what had happened, the shepherd felt sorry for him and said,

- There is a city on the other side of that mountain. It is the city of "*Aiwallah*" (i.e. we accepted by Allah – t.n). Whatever you buy is free on the condition that you say *Aiwallah*.
- Did you say "free"?
- It is free for whom pronounces "*Aiwallah*"

The dervish thought that he was kidding. The shepherd added:

- There are three rules in the city of "*Aiwallah*". If you violate them, you will be expelled from the city.
- What are those rules?
- Firstly, you should not interfere with the work of anyone. Secondly, you should not interfere with divine decrees. Thirdly, you should never lie.
- That's easy. I have already been trained at the dargah; I will not violate these simple rules.

The dervish entered the city hesitatingly and wanted to understand if the shepherd was right. He went to a bath and had a bath there. Then he came to the owner of the bath and said "*Aiwallah*" as his right hand was on his chest. The owner of the bath also said, "*Aiwallah*".

- How much should I pay?
- *Aiwallah* brother, you do not owe anything. You said *Aiwallah*.

The dervish was surprised but he was happy at the same time. He went to the bakers' and saw that they did not demand any money from those who said "*Aiwallah*". The dervish thought, "It was good to be expelled from the *dargah*; for, everything was free in this city. I may live here like a sultan".

A month passed and the dervish enjoyed life there. Meeting one of his friends by chance he said.

- I want to have a family. What should I do to marry a woman?
- Say "*Aiwallah*"
- Just an "*Aiwallah*"?
- Of course. There will be a slave bazaar tomorrow. Go there early. There are beautiful woman from all countries such as Persia, Arabic countries, India, Greece, etc. Choose whomever you desire. Just say "*Aiwallah*" to the merchant.

The dervish did what he was told. He married a week later; the dervish was wandering in the bazaar. There were two women coming ahead: one was young and the other one was old. The young one was almost naked. The other one wore a robe and only her eyes were visible.

The dervish shouted

- Look at this one. Look at her... The parts to be covered are uncovered. Although the old woman does not have to cover all parts, her entire body is covered. Why are you dressed in such a manner?
- When the young women screamed, "Help", the police officer came.
- What's the matter?
- This man is interfering with our business.

The dervish was hit ten strikes at the police station. When he left the police station, he was angry with the fact that he was complained about for warning a fault of a servant and was beaten at the police station. He spoke aloud:

- Oh Allah, what kind of situation is this? I warned the people and I was beaten. Oh, Lord! what kind of thing is it?

A man who heard what the dervish screamed,

- Police, police. When the police officer came there, he said:

- What's happening here?

- This dervish interfered with the work of Allah. Again, they took him to the police station and beat him ten times with a stick. He arrived home with difficulty and went to bed. His door was knocked half an hour later. His wife opened the door. His hunting friends came. They asked his wife if he was home and if he wanted to go hunting with them. His wife entered the room and said,

- Your friends are here. They wanted to ask if you would go hunting with them.
- Tell them that I am not here.
- Police!police
- What's the matter?
- My husband wanted me to tell a lie. He is a liar.

The dervish was deported from the city by police officers. He was covered with dust. He looked at the city and moaned,

- If you do not know the balance of *Aiwallah*, you would say *Aywah* (woe on me).

The sages are both pure and purifiers.

When we arrived at Aksaray, we were all tired, thus we went into an inn. Sultan Walad sent one of the dervishes to Konya to tell them that we were approaching. A few dervishes sat around me as I was sitting in the balcony. It was obvious that they were in a hurry to ask some questions but they were holding back. They told Sultan Walad.

- We wonder if he would answer our questions. And he said,

- There is no reason to feel shame before our Pir from Tabriz. Haven't you seen how great he is during this journey? You can ask your questions to him without hesitation.

- Oh Master, how is it to miss Allah?

- If people are to miss Allah, they should make a distinction between Him and everything other than him. The key for human love and perfectness is a sagacious heart that can see Allah among the chaotic multiplicity of creation. Adam becomes a model for lovers.

In reality, love removed the brilliance of both worlds. The paradise and the hell have a value in the world of servitude. However, they are worth nothing in the realm of love. They gave eight paradises to Adam who was chosen. He sold them for a wheat seed. He burdened the matter of yearning on the camel of fate and came down to the world of grief.

"Oh Adam, what's the value of entering paradise for you?"

Adam said,

"For a person fears Hell, Paradise is worth a thousand bodies; however, for one who is afraid of you, paradise isn't worth a seed of wheat." Then the important thing in Adam being taken from Paradise is to express his yearning.

What makes Adam great is the notion that he carried the trust, which is the love of Allah. Only he knew the limit of love; for, love was the reason lying under his existence. He knew that his love would be nourished only when he tasted the pain of separation. For this reason, he ate from the forbidden fruit.

Generousness and openhandedness sent Adam to Paradise; he sat on the cushion of dignity. The entire Paradise was submitted to his service. He watched the paradise but saw no traces of love and an atom of suffering. He said, "Oil and water cannot be mixed up."

- Then oh Master, how was our father Adam forgiven?
- Oh dervish! You should not think that Adam was taken from paradise due to eating the seed of wheat. He did not violate any decree. Allah's decree was beyond being violated. Allah will accept thousands of people who committed great sins. Is it possible that Allah takes Adam out of the paradise due to an act of rebelling? The fall of Adam is due to a shame for love. The world itself is a shame and thus everything in it is the same.

The essence of the path that leads forgiveness is love and Sufism is the path of love. It is difficult to define love via words. It is like defining honey to a person who has not tasted it. This person cannot know what honey is.

Love is to see goodness and beauty in everything. It is to take lessons by seeing everything as an object lesson, to see the generosity and blessing of Allah on everything and to be grateful for everything bestowed by Allah.

- What should we do if suffering on the way of love leads us to rebel?

- Love is a special suffering that has an excellent taste. Only those who carry this suffering in their hearts may know it. Those who carry this pain can see that everything is Truth and everything leads to the All-Truth. They also know that there is no existent other than the Truth. In the process of conceiving this truth, the lovers extinct in Truth and immerse into the ocean of Truth. Whatever you taste from love can be only a small part of divine love whatever form and level it has. The love between a man and a woman is a part of divine love. However, this worldly love can be a veil before love and the means that lead to love. Surely, this veil would be removed one day and the real Beloved that is the real purpose would be manifested.

The most important thing is to carry this love in the heart in any case. Nevertheless, it is also important to be loved. To love is easier than to be loved. But if you are a lover, you will certainly attain the Beloved one day.

- Who is the cup and who is the wine in the council of love?

- The spiritual Masters are the cupbearers and the dervishes are cups. Love is the essential wine. The cups, that is to say, the seekers are filled by the cupbearer. However, this is the short cut. For, love can be presented to man by other means. As we said, this is the shortest way.

- One of the dervishes asked me whether the love of dervishes for their spiritual master could be regarded a sample of worldly love. In order to understand the relation between a dervish and his shaykh it is not enough to look at this world only, it is also necessary to take the hereafter into consideration.

Zulaikha sacrificed all her properties such as money, fame and rank for the sake of her love for Joseph. She was lost in her love so much that she gave expensive jewelry to those who saw Joseph or who gave any news concerning him. This event became the greatest scandal of Egyptian aristocracy; a woman whom loved her husband's slave without shame.

There is a great truth here. It was not as ordinary love. It had some mysterious things in it. Such a love may let you forget who you are. It protects you from the customs and disapproval of the society in which you live.

The positions of Joseph and *Zulaikha* turned to be just the opposite years later. Joseph became the chief advisor to Pharaoh, that's to say, the second important person in the country. On the other hand, Zulaikha was begging and earning her life through doing difficult jobs.

One day, Joseph was riding his beautiful horse in silk robes together with his advisors and soldiers. He met Zulaikha by chance in the street. Zulaikha was in a terrible condition. The past years removed her beauty. Joseph said:

"Zulaikha, it was impossible for me to marry you when you demanded so in those days; for, you were my master's wife. Now, you are free and I am not a slave. If you wish, I may marry you now."

Zulaikha looked at him and a different light shone in her eyes. "No Joseph, my love for you was only a veil between me and the real Beloved. Praise be to Allah that I removed that veil. Now that I found the real love, I do not need yours."

Zulaikha attained the real love that we seek through her great love for Joseph.

- Oh master, what are the features those corrupt the hearts? We sometimes discuss it. However, we cannot come to a conclusion concerning these features. We would be glad to learn your opinions.

- Your hearts are dead due to ten evil traits. "Allah does not accept the prayers of dead hearts." These ten evil traits are:

1- You claim that you know Allah, but you do not pay your debt. Pay your debt by helping the poor and the needy.

2- You recite the Holy Quran but you are not aware of the laws and decrees. Fulfill what you read.

3- You claim that Satan is your enemy but you obey it. You should reject its offers.

4- You regard yourselves among the *Ummah* of Prophet Mohammad; however, you do not practice his Tradition.

5- You say you wish to enter the Paradise but you do not commit the deeds necessary to enter it.

6- You want to be saved from the fire, but you sometimes drag yourself into it via your evil deeds.

7- You know that everybody will die but you never prepare for it.

8- You see the faults of all your religious brothers but do not see your own faults.

9- You devour all the sustenance from Allah without being grateful and you use all of them without praising. However, you do not give alms to the needy from the sustenance you were bestowed and show your gratefulness.

10- You bury dead ones without learning any lessons despite knowing that you will have the same end.

The prophets and the saints are like mirrors: as the mirrors show the imperfectness on our faces, the friends of Allah show you your faults.

- We heard that you get your name from the *Sura al-Shams*. Could you tell us what is to be understood in this verse. "He who purifies it (the self) has succeeded".

- The soul does not belong to this world. It is of Divine Realm. When the soul enters the body, it is as if imprisoned in a cage. It leads a prison life there. There are organs those enable us to commit various things in our body such as the heart. Since there is no power to put these physical motives into action in the body, it is supported by the soul. The power is in the soul, but the means are in the body.
- When the soul puts these means into undesired actions, then the qualities of soul become obvious. Allah never created anything ugly and bad.The ugly and bad are the violations we commit by our humane will.

Who is responsible for our bad deeds in this case? The soul? On the Last Day, the body will blame the soul saying "I had no power to commit evil" and the soul would blame the body saying, "I had no means to commit evil". Their blames will be answered as such: you are like a blind man and a paralyzed person who helped each other in evil. The paralyzed had ability to see and decide to commit evil. Both of them were guilty.

The self is not evil in itself. Do not blame your self. An important aim of Sufi training is to raise the level of the self; you are surrounded by the passions of body and lust. You get annoyed with yourself when you realize the evil you committed on the second level and try to commit everything for the sake of Allah whether good or evil on the next level.

Allah says, "We blew him from our soul." It is this soul that is imprisoned in the body until the command of "Turn to your Lord" at the moment of death. The lowest levels of soul do not want to leave the body. As they became a part of the body, they reject leaving there.

- How about the souls of prophets and saints?
- Their souls are completely different than ours. They are purer. The worldly substances on the bodies of these

perfect men were taken from the most sacred and pure parts of the world. As their bodies do not commit evil and are completely pure, the soul will not be impure when it enters them; "One who knows his soul knows his lord" is known almost by everyone. It has two meanings:

Firstly, we know our needs, passions and weakness; in addition to these, we believe in Allah who has infinite Power. Then we know that we need a Protector who feeds, shelters and dresses us in the world. The second one is a mysterious explanation. Allah says, "We are nearer than your jugular veins". We begin explaining this profound relation with Allah during the stage of knowing ourselves. We attain The Truth using this relation. To return to Allah in this world is possible only by following His commands before we die. Those who do not follow Allah and obey Satan will be separated.

Think of a bunch of grapes. Each grape torn from the bunch will go off; but those who remain together live longer. The grape will be nourished as long as it remains in the bunch. All the things are the same and beautiful from the point of essence. It is only the outward qualities that are ugly.

- Do our dreams consist of the images during the journey of our souls?
- Like the light that emerges from the candle, the soul leaves the body in order not to cut the relations off. This light stretches to the *Lawh-i Mahfudh* and "reads" the parts concerning itself. When it wakes up, the soul returns to the body just as one turns off a torch. As a result of stretching beyond, we may learn something that is impossible to be within our knowledge. However, what we learn as such is only a part of divine knowledge.

There are objects and symbols in dreams; and only the real wise people can read them; but the meaning derived from these symbols may vary from level to level, person to person and from soul to soul.

- Are the souls also various as we are?

- Everybody has seven souls. The mineral soul, the vegetative soul, the animal soul, the human soul, the angelic soul, the mysterious soul of mystery. The symbols vary depending on the level of soul they attached and on the person who sees them and the soul that conceives them. A sultan may have the same dream as his servant, but their meanings are different. It is important that which level of soul sees the dream. The dreams seen by the animal soul and vegetative soul reflect the motives and the desires of the self. For instance, if you sleep hungry, you will see yourself eating food. The human soul sees symbols. As an instance, a snake may mean properties; but if a dervish sees it, it may be an allusion to the lowest self.

- Which one is better, to be a theologian or to be a saint?

- If it was possible to learn spirituality (the knowledge of God) via listening and training, then Bayazid and Junayd would have to spill earth on their heads before Fahr al-Din Razi out of grief and be a student of him at least for a hundred years. According to an account, Fahr al-Din Razi wrote a book consisting of almost a thousand pages on Quranic interpretation. However, a hundred thousand *Razi*s cannot reach an atom of dust in Bayazid's street. Razi is the one who knocks the door outside. He cannot reach inside. For, that door is opened only for exclusive friends. The ones who stay outside cannot step in.

The miracles of some saints are secret. They cannot veil the secrets due to their secrecy. Let me tell you a few stories concerning this matter:

Bayazid used to go for pilgrimage on foot. He went for pilgrimage seventy times. One day, he saw that people were miserable and scattered due to the lack of water. There was a dog near a well; as the pilgrims were crowded around the well, it could not reach water. When the dog looked at him, Bayazid had a divine inspiration, "Go and get some water for the dog". He immediately said, "I will give an accepted and pure pilgrimage in return for a bowl of water". Nobody cared. He went on increasing the amount. "Six or seven pilgrimages that was fulfilled on foot". There was no answer. When Bayazid said, "I will give seventy pilgrimages", a man accepted the offer. In the meantime, Bayazid thought "How blessed I am (what a good person I am). I sold all my pilgrimages for the sake of a dog". He poured some water into the bowl any gave it to the dog, but it turned its face. Then Bayazid repented and he was inspired, "For how long will you say I did this and that for Allah boastingly? As you see, the dog did not accept your water". He cried and said, "I regret and repent, I will not think as such anymore". Then the dog turned to him and began drinking the water.

- Master, sometimes we happen to fear from death. We feel shame and it does not behoove a dervish to fear. How can we overcome it?

- Our prophet said, "The believers do not die but they are moved." That is to say, death and moving are different things. For instance, suppose that you are in a narrow and dark house and you cannot move there; you cannot hold your legs ahead; but if you are moved to a mansion that has a big garden, can this be called death? My words are a clear as mirrors. If you have illumination and intuition in you, may you desire death (do not fear death). May Allah help you! We congratulate you! Do not forget to pray for us. If you do not possess such an intuition and passion, then form such a desire, look and try for it; for, there is information in Quran concerning this matter: "Say (unto them): If the abode of the Hereafter in the providence of Allah is indeed for you alone and not for others of mankind (as ye pretend), then long for death (for ye must long for death) if ye are truthful." (2:94). There are certainly ones who have such a sincere faith among men and women. May these words be a mirror for you so that you may see your own condition in it. Whatever work you commit is regarded as good unless you hate death. If you hesitate to do something, look at this mirror and make a decision. Prepare yourself for death under a brilliant light and wait or gain this state by your efforts just like those who try to do it.

The brave person is one who knows how to be happy when he is sorrowful and cheerful, when he is distressed; for, aims are hidden in aimlessness. There are many hopes in hopelessness, but to be anxious immediately is the main hopelessness. I was happy when I was sick; for, I knew that I would get well soon; and I may be sick soon when I am healthy, I was anxious about this issue. As you know, some people say, "If I had not eaten it, I would have been sick today". They seek consolation in these words. However, the brave one is whom can endure any kind of trouble; his nobility lies here. He becomes perfect in this way.

- Do you think knowing the Truth is easier than to knowing people?
- To understand these people is more difficult than to understand Allah. For example, when you see a piece of wood carved well, you may imagine its carver; for, that wood cannot become as such by itself. When you look at people, they may resemble you outwardly; but you cannot know their inward. They may be far from your imagination and thought. Looking at a processed piece of wood, you can grasp the mastery of the artisan, but only the perfect ones can conceive the broadness of that art.
- Oh dervishes, you asked me many questions. Now let me ask you a question.

- Of course, master! But everyone knows that your questions are harder than the trump of doom.
- Why do you cry?
- ...
- Let me give you the answer by the story of a dervish.

A Sufi was in search of divine mystery for years and tried to attain it a lot. Wherever he found a saint or a shaykh, he served him but could not attain what he sought, as it was not the right time. The gate of meaning could not open unto him.

"Whatever work you have, if it is not time
It is not beneficial for you, whomsoever your friend is."

He went to a graveyard one day. He remembered his quest and began crying. Then he put his head on a brick and fell asleep. He woke up and took that brick. He took it with him wherever he went: to the bath, mosque, toilet, *sama*, bazaar and everywhere else. He used to kiss the brick and something put it on his head. One day, a man asked, "Why don't you put that brick aside?" He said, "I will take it to the grave and make it my cushion. I had lost one of my qualities for a long time; I was hopeful and then lost that hope afterwards. When I put this brick under my head, I attained what I sought." The Holy Prophet said, "If someone attains divine Bliss, he should be attached to it then."

A man died. They called a lamenter. The lamenter asked his relatives:

- What was his skill? Did he have knowledge? They said, "No". "Then was he pious?" They said, "No". The lamenter turned to the direction of *qibla* and asked, "Did he help the poor and the needy?" They said, "No". He got a negative answer for all his questions. Then the lamenter began crying.

"Oh the one who came confused and who left confused; who was born confused and who died confused!"

- Now, are you one of the dervishes who draws a lesson from the brick or the confused one whom the lamenter was crying for?

THE WELLCOMING FEAST

There is no need for expressing; my condition is obvious for you.
There is no need for tongue; my silence is a statement for you
There is no need for words; my quietness is speaking for you
There is no need for speaking, love is moaning for you

It was spring in Konya but this spring was a false one. They were only shadows that gathered only to please Mawlana unwillingly. They thought of a magnificent and crowded welcoming. Mawlana prevented them and said:

- Shams is not a king or sultan. We, the lovers of Truth are strangers like prophets and our hearts suffer from luxury. The *jamra*s (any of the three increase of heat that are supposed to effect first air, then water and finally the earth according to customs –t.n) fell first on air, then on water and on earth at last. Yet, there was a fourth one that was the *jamra* of love. It fell on Mawlana's heart as an eyelash and heated him. He had a smile on his face, which had not smiled for months. For, his beloved was on the way. The corn roses of night spread around all the streets of the city. The yellow wild flowers rose towards the blue sky among the corn roses; they smelled wonderfully. Mawlana was moving up and fro like the children on the days of religious festivals. He almost lost his strength because of coming in and going out many times. He said to the disciple next to him:

- We will get him seated on the wooden sofa under the oak tree in your garden; and listen to the memories of longing from him in joy.

He had a different sight of joy in his eyes. His disciples were even more cheerful than he was as they saw their master happy whom they had not seen smiling for months.

Those scholars, who criticized me harshly first in their sermons and meetings at home blamed me for heresy and even went further by blaming me of disbelief, offered Mawlana to organize a splendid welcoming only to ingratiate themselves with Mawlana. He said:

- He is not a king. We are lovers of Allah and we are strange prophets. We want neither your presents nor applauses.

Then the caravan came to Zincirli Inn near Konya to welcome me. In the meantime, Sultan Walad sent one of his dervishes to give the good news of our coming to Mawlana.

Mawlana gave whatever he had with him to the herald. He told them to give him more and read one of his best *ghazals*:

Spill water on the roads
Give the good news to the gardens
The smell of spring is approaching
He is coming!
Our brilliant moon, soul and beloved is coming,
Let him pass, give way and open the road
Stand away, away from the way
His face is luminous, pure
Illumining where he steps
He is coming!

Everybody said altogether, "He is coming!" This sentence made pink moire reflections on pale skins and town criers were shouting on the streets. "Shams is coming!" Then Shams came. Mawlana was speaking like a roaring lion.

Oh friends, my sun and moon has come
My argent bodied
My eyes and ears have come.
I am intoxicated
And cheerful inside.
The walking cypress has come
From whom I died until mornings
And spilt on the road like a bunch of rose
Look for the sake of Allah
Look at the joy of this spring…
Oh sun, open thyself entirely
Generous as my beloved
The power in my body
Will spring like a seed
It is just the right time of roaring
My lion has come.
The distress received, the pains forgotten one by one
Who is like a rose!
Who is like sugar and money
My beloved has come.
Oh Shams Tabrizi!
Oh the light in my eyes!
They took me from myself
Then everything will be settled
My pierced skinned friend
And argent bodied friend
My heart, beloved has come.

Hope is the only consolation. One who knows to hope is familiar with the mystery in attainment. The smell of Shams came even before him. It tasted like the rain. Steppes inhaled this smell. Then the travellers appeared far away. It was almost evening and that place had the hunger for love.

Mawlana was waiting for us at the city border together with some notable people. Sultan Walad was holding the bridle of my horse. I was riding slowly as my head was lowered and my black robe was floating by the wind. I dismounted from the horse. As my friend was waiting for me standing for hours, my feet should be in a hurry like *buraq*. As I came nearer, I heard the heart beats of the beloved. It was as if the stars in the sky would come down out of respect during the day. We embraced each other… We both burst into tears. We were trying to remove tears dropping from our cheeks. I missed his smell. I heard his moaning so deep that it was as if my lungs would be drowned in their own blood. We embraced each other so long. His chest was so hot. I whispered in his ears, "Mirages are false and the water flows into the ocean of secrets." Also he whispered that the rose was waiting for earth for a long time, it dreamed its rain and missed the sun madly.

The same thing occurred years ago in the middle of the bazaar in Konya. I stopped Mawlana and held the bridle of his horse. Now it was Mawlana who was holding the bridles. The two oceans met once again, a second *maraj al-bahrayn*" (the meeting of the seas).

As this secret scene occurred, the ones who memorized Quran were reciting the Holy Book and the disciples were whirling. The sounds of the *nay* and the *qudum* were aloud. Mawlana helped me dismount. We kissed each other's hands as the friends of Allah. We kept silent for a while and spoke in the spiritual language.

I told about the service and kindness of Sultan Walad during the journey:

- I have two innate states: one of them is my head and the other one is my secret. I sacrificed my head and the other one is my secret. I sacrificed my head on your way in full sincerity. I gave my secret to Walad. If our son Walad had a life as long as that of Noah and spent it on worshipping and self-denial, he would not gain any secret as big as the one I gave to him.

In fact, during the journey that lasted one month, Sultan Walad cared for me as he protects his eyes and exerted great effort to make sure I had an easy journey. I tried to ornament his heart and I gave him my secrets during our conversations:

"Son, Mawlana's dearest one is also a rose for me. You are my son. Time trips away and I may leave this world when the time comes and also your father dies; but inscribe my advices unto your heart."

Liars are not faithful. How can the repenting of an immoral one remain firm? The mean ones have little loyalty.

You'd better regard the hypocrites as your enemies. Keep away from them and their actions.

Demand only lawful sustenance to let the religion remain pure and genuine. The heart of the person who wants unlawful sustenance is doomed for death in his body. The greatest catastrophe is not to know the source of them.

I understand that you have a desire to write, but do not write anything, not even two lines as long as I am alive. Take your pen after I pass away; whenever your inspiration ceases and your pen stops, wear this ring; the name of this agate ring is *ibtida* (the beginning), thus your book's title would be *Ibtidanama*

- All right my dear Pir. I need your advices, which will be a sparkle to write my book.
- Then, listen to me son! May these advices be light for you:

"To train the dervishes is like growing up a chaste girl. You need to be careful concerning where they go or with whom they meet. Their meeting with wrong people is like sowing bad seeds on a pure field; it is not possible to harvest good crops there.

Do not submit yourself immediately about the issues on love; when you submit yourself, you will submerge into depths.

The illuminated ones cannot be the captives of officials. If people are determined, they may overcome the fate; when the will is intensified, it can impel energy. The illuminated people do not allow customs to put them in a pattern.

When you commit an evil and if you fear that people will find out, then that evil has goodness in it. When you commit goodness, and want people to hear about it, it has an evil in it.

The eyes and ears, the sight and hearing are outward grabbers; but if the inward falcon is sober and standing and is staying indifferent among all of them, the grabbers can change and become members of household.

When you meet some silent and incomprehensible people, do not unveil your thoughts to them. When you meet egoist and touchy people, beware of your words.

Those who trust others will see that some people are not sincere; but they remain sincere. Those who doubt about others will see that not everyone betrayed them; but they remain always in betrayal.

To commit goodness and not to profit from it is like a pumpkin that grows among grass; it grows inconspicuously.

To commit evil and not to stay damaged is like the spring snow in the garden; it will inevitably either melt or vapor up.

Zeal is to be careful concerning virtues and justice; however, the worldly people use any zeal to solve their economic problems. Simplicity is not to be interested in material properties; however, the worldly people use simplicity to cover their stinginess. In this way, the principles of illuminated life become means for the private works of small people. What a pity!

The objectors and slanderers are like the pieces of cloud that cover the sun temporarily; it will be sunny soon. Flatterers are like the current of air that sticks into the skin; the person will be harmed without discrimination…

Now that you cannot cook the raw
Then do not make the cooked one raw...

We entered the *dargah* with Mawlana hand in hand. We missed each other so much that we smelled each other's scent for minutes. We continued our conversations from where we had left them; we enjoyed ourselves in the council of love jumping from one conversation to another. We began to remove our longing via our *halwah*s.

If I had not come here, Mawlana would have been a light known only in Konya or a river that flows only on this arid field. I will announce my beloved to the world; I will make him an ocean.

People were happy with Mawlana as such. However, God (Mawla) was not happy with Mawlana.

- Why are you preaching in the mosque? Why do you caress their ears, not their hearts?
- To let people be educated.
- You have been preaching for years. Then who changed and what is the reality?
- We do not know it.

Who will know it? You do not know people. Change your preaching tomorrow. Stop telling tender anecdotes. Tomorrow, give your sermon on hell; add some bitterness in your words. Complain about the court and dramatize your sermon. Let your words be severe and sharp. You will see that the audience will grow bigger tomorrow. The public enjoys crying ones and the preaching that makes them cry. However, they cannot even cry.

You have to preach tomorrow. This is a hard task. The gates are open, if you do not preach, they will shout and exclaim around. If only they benefit from your sermons. Although all words are uttered in an obvious manner, they cannot let them conceive the purpose of the words as if they have not been admonished before. Now that they understand it not, then how will they practice it? The result of unconscious acts is heresy. What is the worth of words that come out of the mouth only?

Tell them about the paradise on the third day. Speak peacefully. You will see that many people want paradise but they do not desire it. Your words would be like lying for them. Try and you will see. Then stop preaching. Come and I will give you the greatest of all preaching aloud.

You cannot go beyond *Sidrat al-Muntaha* unless you read your own heart. There is only Allah beyond. There has never been anything in the world other than Allah. Only the eyes were mistaken. ..The intellect thought it could know everything. It could not know even itself.

If the pen had not written the heart, the words would have been as decors in your mouth. Only loneliness may fill empty words.

Can love be lived without daring to die? Isn't it only a word between love and death? Then what is the expected word? Here is the secret. The "word" finished and "state" started. We entered in that state. We meet our humane secret during our *Asma al- Huthna* (the beautiful names of Allah t.n) invocation. We never left Allah whether in Paradise or in the world. We never left that state by our own state.

- You will look at people in a different manner after me. Your sight would grow you in the hearts. The four walls, four gates, and Konya is not your right place and audience.

Ignorance is surely better a hundred times
Than the knowledge that does not take you from yourself

I prayed the Morning Prayer. Mawlana entered in while I was reciting the Quran. Mawlana said,

- What will you serve today? I used to begin the day by *Asrarnama*.

- Why are you always talking about the books? Why are you repeating the words of others? Don't you have your own words?

- All right, Shams! Do you know the Sultan of Sages?

- Who is he?

- Muhyiddin ibn al-Arabi

- Forget about what he said. He gains his dead knowledge from the dead ones; but I gain my knowledge from the ever living one.

- The sage is who never stops remembering the friend and is never contented with his friendship. There is no food sweeter than the invocation, which enters in the mouth of certainty on the table of contentment.

- The spiritual knowledge is gained through three things. The invoking tongue, the praising heart and the skin that is patient. The body without knowledge is like a city with no water. Finally, it is a dry form. It is necessary to adorn the body with abstinence, morality, educating the self heartily.

- Adorn me with your wisdom, my dear Shams.

- I say "light" and you understand it as mud. I invite you to love but you send me into fire. In fact, I have burning in fire in my destiny; but if you refuse to burn in greater fires than that of yours, why should I burn? I say love and you say, "May it be Love". I say the heart but you follow the shadows. Settle down oh my heart; I should have trouble that I may not change it with remedy. Tell me, are you trouble?

To be Friend is to be the rose
Together with leaves and thorns

Mawlana, you are a rose; for this reason, I travelled from city-to-city and put my head on your knees. Let me tell you the reason why you are a rose.

- I would be glad to hear that.
- There is a story about a dervish. One day a dervish came to Anatolia from Horasan to find a new *dargah* for himself. He knocked the door of a *dargah* in Sivas…
- In the meantime, the shaykh was conversating with his disciples; he shouted to the disciple who was going towards the door before he opened it. "Stop my dear son. There is a dervish behind the door. This is certain from the way he knocked… I understand his intention. Bring me a glass before I give an answer." The shakyh filled the glass with water fully. "Now give this glass to the dervish at the door. He will understand my message." The message was as follows:
- Oh son, our *dargah* is full of students. There is no place for you. If we accept you, we cannot show you a place. We have no place. We have no place even for one. Go and find another place. The dervish took a leaf from a rose in the garden and put it on the glass. However, the water did not spill out. The dervish said:
- Now, take this glass to the shaykh. He will understand what I meant and aimed to say. The shaykh understood him seeing that the water did not spill out despite the leaf on it.

The dervish said:

- Oh master, oh pir! Accept me to your *dargah*; I am a petal from a rose; the rose does not cause trouble but removes it; allow me in, I will not cause a problem here. Do not deprive me of the smell of your wisdom and your water of service.

- A real friend should be secret like Allah. One should tolerate the evil sides and unpleasant features of a friend; and he should not be hurt by his faults. He should not leave and object the friend. In fact, Allah never leaves his servant due to their failings, sins, and imperfectness. He gives sustenance with full mercy and blessing; this is friendship without rancor and grudge.

I was carrying on with my teaching on one hand and trying to ripen Mawlana during the spiritual trainings that continued for nights. Mawlana was ready for this process and he even went further beyond me. He said in one of his *ghazals*:

- A moon appeared at dawn; it descended and began looking at us just like a falcon that hunted a bird under moonlight. The moon caught me and flew upwards. I looked at myself but could not see me. For, my body turned into a soul by the bliss of that moon. I went to the realm of souls. I saw nothing other than the moon there. In short, the secrets of eternal manifestation were totally understood.

In another *ghazal*, Mawlana explains this change by the following verses:

- Your love made me intoxicated. I began clapping. I was drunk and unconscious; I did not know what I was doing. I was an unripe grape but I became a ripen one now. I cannot show myself as sour faced. The public said, "One should not be like that". I am not like that; he made me as such. Again:

- I was as ascetic and resisted like a mountain. But is there a mountain drags you like a straw although it knows you very well?. To praise you is the praising of one himself. For, one who praises the sun is, in fact, praising himself…

- I told Mawlana that he and his friends should give whatever they have for the love and for the sake of the beloved.

Mawlana was surprised. He said:

- I did not understand.

I said;

- Let me tell you the story of Prophet Ibrahim (Abraham); when Allah saved him from Nimrod's fire, he sacrificed a thousand rams, three hundred oxen and a hundred camels as an expression of his gratitude. No one has ever heard or seen such a generosity.
- When they asked why he sacrificed all these, he answered that he would even sacrifice himself for Him. "Isn't it normal that I sacrificed them? It is Allah who possesses me and all that I have. The things I sacrificed are nothing. I would sacrifice the dearest things I had for the sake of Allah. For example, if I had a son, I might sacrifice even my son if Allah wishes me to do."

The disciples of Bayazid-i Bistami complained to him about Satan and said, "Satan takes our faith". The shaykh called the Satan and questioned it. Satan said,

- I can never force anyone to do something. I fear Allah so much that I dare not to do it. In fact, the majority of people leave their faith for simple things. All I do is to collect the thrown faith…

Satan also has all human features except for one: it does not know love. Love was not given to it; it was given to the sons of Adam.

Allah told Gabriel (*Jibril*), "Oh Gabriel! How would you worship Me if I created you as a man?"

"Oh, Lord! You know everything that has happened, that will happen, and that is likely to happen. Nothing on heavens and earth is hidden from You. You also know how I would worship You"

Allah said, "I know, oh *Jibril*! However, my servants know that not. Tell them so that they may hear and learn!"

Jibril said, "Oh Lord! If I were a man, I would worship you in three ways: firstly, I would quench the thirst of thirsty ones. Secondly, I would veil the faults of those who committed faults. And thirdly I would help the poor". Then Allah said, "I know that you would do all these. Thus, I assigned you as the bearer of my commands and send you to the messengers".

Satan has all human features but one
Love is the only bliss that it lacks
What Satan envies man due to the lack of his love.

Satan has never seen paradise. The serpent in paradise was something beautiful: it had four legs... But after the events Adam experienced, Allah took its legs off and commanded it to crawl. Its skin is used for bags and shoes for women. That snake was not Satan but it was necessary for that event to take place. Adam should have eaten the fruit from the forbidden tree: so, Allah placed Satan at the end of the serpent's mouth for a single moment.

There is a subtle wisdom here: Satan was the poison, not the serpent. It was not even the tongue. It was only the poison on the serpent's tongue. This is a sign that Satan is what makes us astray at the end of our tongues.

Allah said when He was expelling Adam from paradise: "Be the enemy of each other by backbiting and cursing".

Satan used to be an angel; it was even the teacher of Angels. Its real name was *Kharis* (the ambitious). It had a great ambition for worshiping Allah. There was no place in the universe, which it had not prostrated. However, when Allah created Adam, it thought its worshiping maintained it a privilege. It became arrogant and thus rejected the prostrate before Adam when Allah ordered it to do so. Its arrogance due to its past worshiping caused it to be expelled from paradise and far from divine mercy.

When Allah ordered it to leave paradise and go to hell, it said it worshipped Him for thousands of years and wanted respite.

Allah gave a respite until the last day. Satan expressed that it would deceive people within this respect and try to make them astray. It said, "I would be on their right and left sides, at the back and front of them."

Allah permitted it but he also added, "I will throw all your followers into the hell and I will manifest Myself above and below my servants".

As you see, Satan took four directions but left above and below for Allah. For this very reason, we raise our hands for praying and put our head down for prostration.

One day, the Shaykh of Ahi Muhammad Diwana, As al-Din Mutakallim was interpreting the following verse to the disciples of Mawlana in Sivas: "and He is with you wheresoever ye may be" (57: 4). I could not help listening and asked a question to the Shaykh.

- How can servants be together with Allah?

- Man of Tabriz! What is your real intention with this question?

Nevertheless, he was behaving in a mild manner while showing his anger.

- I am here; does this make any sense? There is no grudge in this question. You are a dog tied from its tongue which has adopted the way of oppressing as a habit. You say, "Allah is together with you" and I said how can He be together with the servants.

- Yes, Allah is together with his slave by his knowledge.

- But knowledge is not separate from the essence. Moreover, no attribute is separate from the essence.

- You ask old questions.

- What does "old" mean? These are fresh ones.

- Then he could not utter anything and the only thing he could do was lowering his head as a sign of respect.

The public said, "This is a theologian" but most of them adopted his opinions.

THE LADY WHO TURNED MY CHEMISTRY (KIMIYA) UPSIDE DOWN

I learned the taste of love from Mawlana
and the overflowing of it from Kimya

Konya was just as I left it before. It was in a deep silence. It seemed to be in a peace of the silence whereas it was unwillingly as if saying, "Let's give Shams a last chance" for the sake of Mawlana. The public and scholars had an attitude of sacrificed slaves thrown before lions in an arena against me. I did not care about their careful posture or them seeing me as dynamite about to explode. If to love is kissing with dynamite in your mouth, then exploding or dispersing does not matter for me. I came there for Mawlana. It was not me that needed to change and I did not owe them anything. I told Mawlana, "I came here for you, not for Konya. If they had told me that your father would have come to life again if you came from Tabriz, I would not have moved by Allah. Do not expect me to tolerate them; I would be even worse than before. It is difficult to live with me. I told you before. Shams is the same as in the past and in the future.

Mawlana had a tendency to keep me in Konya until the end of my life. He wanted me to marry, to arrange a house and thus to settle in Konya permanently. Mawlana knew Konya and its citizens very well. They were likely to criticize me again one day. The world was full of unripen people. They would not understand such a divine conversation and they were not a society that would be ripen in these councils and conversations.

They saw only the outward of things and wanted to the possess Mawlana. They thought that everything would be settled if Shams left the city. However, this was not the case. Mawlana needed me as soul and spirit. To separate us was like separating the soul from the body. But who would understand this? Mawlana feared to lose me again for this reason and was looking for ways to let me stay in Konya. He knew that I would not return to Konya if I left once again.

He had an adopted daughter who grew up in his house, trained, adorned; she had exoteric and esoteric morality and was beautiful. Moreover, she had richness of heart and purity that behooves to Sufis. Mawlana treated her just as he treated his own children and liked her as his own daughter. He wanted me to marry her and in this way to settle in Konya. He also had some uncertainties. Firstly, he was not sure whether I would accept the marriage or not. Secondly, I was old and she was young. Thirdly, his son Alaaddin also loved her platonically. Thus, his small son would be an enemy of him. Mawlana was in a dilemma. Another issue was that a few preeminent scholars of Konya also thought of her as a bride for their sons. Mawlana thought on these issues, and finally spoke with Kira Hatun and Sultan Walad concerning this matter. Kira Hatun, who had been careful and calm since the day I came, responded positively in a manner against who would say, "Kira Hatun would oppose this marriage". Sultan Walad said, "Dear Father, you know the best. If you are anxious about my brother, I will persuade him and prevent him from reacting. But we should ask Kimya's opinion first".

Mawlana did not want to get married for a long time after his wife Gawhar Hatun died; however, his admirers helped him to marry Kira Hatun who used to be a Christian widower with her three children. Kira never treated Kimya different from her own children and even liked her more. When she told Kimya about the issue, she kept silent and approved, "My father knows me better than I do". There was no problem for a girl like her who had an education on divinely matters. She would be a woman "of state" (*hâl*) within a short period before my inspiration of love. However, it was not only Alaaddin that hesitated for this marriage; I was also unwilling.

Now the thing was to persuade me for such a marriage. I had never thought about marriage in my whole life. I was almost 68 and never thought of a woman. Mawlana also knew that I did not have such an intention, which made him anxious most. During a conversation he said,

- Oh, Shams! What a good companion is Kimya Hatun, isn't she?

- For whom?

- Of course for you.

- You know me very well. Praise be to the Lord that I have never thought about women until now.

- Did not Allah make women our wives?

- Women are wives for some people and carcass for others.

- Look my dear, Kimya is a young girl and I am one who purified himself from lusts. I will say what Jesus told Mary Magdalena. Mary Magdalene loved Jesus and waited for a proposal from him. Jesus understood the matter and said, "Marriage is a matter of flesh and do not expect for anything about flesh from me".

- I want you not to be alone; I want you to have a friend for conversation. I want someone to pour water for your ablution. Allah bestowed upon us the elegance of women. Companionship cannot occur with body, the affection of heart is sustenance for the soul. My aim was that you might feed my daughter Kimya by your spiritual intuition, oh Shams, and that my dear Kimya would accompany you.

I pondered over Mawlana's words. The skill of persuasion was not by what he said but in what he did not say. "Oh, Shams! You are love for me beyond the universe, you are my beloved; the fear grows again inside me for the possibility of your separation. How can I endure if you go again? If you expel yourself, my exhausted heart would explode. May Kimya be not a bond for you; may my hunger for you attach Kimya's heart to you and may Kimya be a bond for you so that my fears would disappear. Know it well that I am poor and mad; let me give my daughter for you so that the thing I fear may not happen. Accept this marriage to remove my fears and for the sake of your love towards me."

I read the expressions those that resided in the heart of the friend as pains. I would decide only after talking with Kimya.

- If Kimya is contented with this, I accept her. Now that you want to stop the winds, which will certainly blow, then may it be as you wish.

I wanted to talk to Kimya face-to-face. Although I stayed at the *dargah* for years, this was the first time I saw her. I had to understand her opinions concerning me. Only she would heal my discontented side with her answers.

- I know what they told you about me as if I heard with my own ears. I am the one who can read into the ears and the eyes.

- I do not act by the words of others. I am deaf to the outside.

- I appreciate your answer.

- Do not hesitate to ask questions if you have any.

- Why have not you married until now? Didn't you have any passions or desires?

- The reason why I fasted almost every day during my adolescence was to remove the lust that would nourish inside me. I succeeded in doing so; I killed the lust. I never feel any sexual desire for anybody. I do not regard love as passion and I do not veil love with lust. That is why I remained as a bachelor until the age of sixty-eight.

- What do you think of women?

- The reason for not marrying was not my hatred for women or regarding them as the reason of evil. I am not one of those heretics who see them as Satan. They are the trust of Allah. I only kept away from worldly things. I do not think about women, or food, fame or wealth. Many women also loved our Master Jesus, but he abstained from them. I walk in his steps when love is concerned.

- Then what happened to you?

- Your father invited me to the tradition of our Prophet: "Three things were made lovable for me: canonical prayer, beautiful scent and woman."

- What a good invitation it is.

- Both the invitation and the owner of the invitation is beautiful and good.

- You are young and beautiful; although you have many admirers, why did you choose me?

- For sacrifice.

- Sacrifice for what?

- Nothing… Sacrifice... Only for love.

- We both are contented with making Mawlana happy, aren't we?

Kimya was speaking so beautifully that she was like a brilliant spring flowing from the mountain on which snow had just melted. I could not have enough if I listened to her for a whole day. Her voice was either as a rose leaf or morning dew. Her words were as lamenting like the blow of the nay, soft like velvet and warm as tears. Khurshid in Indian and Asian legends was only a blossom compared with Kimya; but I have nothing of Jamshid. I would submit planets before Kimya Hatun. However, the light in the sun is almost extinct. It had been years since I killed the monster of lust inside me. I am not at an age to be busy with women. I kept away from them. I am only a piece of ash since I sent my fire to the sun; a piece of ash, which cannot even fire a piece of paper and which is almost burnt out. I devoted all my belongings to Mawlana. While she spoke, I was wandering in the skies like white cranes. I looked and realized that her sight was fixed on my blue eyes.

- I was a fire that burns, but I am gradually dying away.

- Did you send all your fire to my father?

- No, he was already burning; I only served as the wind. Do you complain like everyone that I changed your father?

- My father is happy with you. I do not complain; on the contrary, I am grateful.

As she was pondering over the depth of devotion, I immersed in thoughts concerning Kimya amidst the silence. Kimya was already young and was like a newly blossomed rose. Many people wanted to marry her. Many teenagers, especially Alaaddin, were burning with her love. She was so beautiful that the roses in the garden would fade with envy. Her forehead was the reflection of the moon and her eyes were as black as the night. Her hair covered her face like forelocks. Her peers envied her beauty. She was like a garden of paradise that had to be protected from the evil eye. She was an example of sacrifice for love. When Mawlana told about his opinions concerning me, she nobly answered with no hesitation: "Dear father, I know your love for him. If you want me to devote myself for your love, know that I may sacrifice a thousand *Kimya*s for you and Shams. I may sacrifice my earthly life for Shams in the same manner as Ismail's submission. And I will do this not only to comfort your heart but also to be honored by attaining both yours and his love which make even the angels envy. I abstained all worldly matters only to benefit from your love; let me be a Zulaikha…"

Although I spoke to her concerning marriage face-to-face, the distress inside me was not over. I was hesitant of making Mawlana sad. I was hesitant for the fear that I might take a false step during the journey of love I carried in my heart for years. I feared to sadden Mawlana, who removed everything on the way of love with a single stroke, who stood against everyone for the sake of his life and who sacrificed everything for the beloved. This is the first time I experienced such a feeling. The brave Shams became a timid gazelle thinking that either he might make Kimya unhappy or the beloved would be grieved. And an undisposed marriage does not bring a dazzling joy with it. I had no beloved other than Mawlana. A planned marriage is like facing the ideal model of the beloved we developed inside us consciously or unconsciously. It was long ago that I closed the doors for women. I put a gate between my heart and my tongue. Kimya could not be acting for the loyalty of promise I gave to love years ago. Moreover, it was as if drowning among the waves I floated between the craziness of age of eighteen and the thirst of sixty – eight whether to love or not. She was the only woman, my only consolation belonging to the heart of my old world that has almost died away. Even while guiding others, man always realizes that he to is guided by another.

I was anxious about whether she would underestimate me or find me weak and cease to love. However, love does not need any masks. I was alone and she loved me obviously. She was obliged to love me; for, she loved and will love only me. .. Kimya, this is your first and the last love. How meaningfully she spoke. Her voice was as clear as the sound of a spring and untouched as the singing of birds. Love really makes one childish. That's to say, it makes one to pretend to believe.

Kimya is the Pleiades in the sky, visible but inaccessible; she is the paradise on earth; admired but not experienced… Kimya possesses the meaning and knows the secret. She has a hunger for divine love in the ocean of spirituality due to her spiritual state of years. She is silent by her thirst. It is as if I was the one whom she waited for. She was busy with prayers and supplications. She fasted-the fast of silence-just as Miriam.

Kimya is a treasure that could hide herself. She kept away from the evil sights. She has such chastity that it is as if she has hidden herself even for women. She turns away from mirrors in the fear of being arrogant with her beauty. Kimya is humble and calm. She is like Fatima who found nobility in piety. She closed her doors to the arrogance of life. Wherever she finds an orphan heart, she caresses the souls by gentle words. As her tears are busy with preparing her dowry, she says, "Is there a dowry better than morality and chastity?"

Kimya is like Hagar who devoted herself entirely to the Creator by her loneliness in the desert. She is like faithful Hadija who said, "Whatever I have is sacrificed in your way" and who believes in what she trusted. Kimya is like Rabia who did not care for worldly affairs, who did not live in imagination and saw the real richness in self-beauty. She is like a noble heroine who never wanted any worldly wealth even in her dreams and has never prayed for herself in her entire life.

Which Kimya could grasp Shams' secret?
Which Kimya (chemistry) would not melt under the sun (Shams)?

It was winter. A curtain divided the entrance of the madrasa and it was turned into two small rooms. After a humble wedding ceremony, this new room was given to the recently married couple. Mawlana recited the prayer of marriage; Husam al-din Chalabi and Sultan Walad were our witnesses. No one talked about *mahr* (a determined amount or valuable material to be given to the bride in case of divorce-t.n.) However, I said,

- Kimya Hatun, I have nothing to give you as *mahr*. All that I have is my servitude and I submitted it to Allah. I would have wanted to say that I sacrificed my head for you; however, I sacrificed it for your father. The only *mahr* I may give you is our love and sharing something. You should know that I have no wealth other than my words. Kimya nodded with her eyes and smiled.

When I entered the room the first night, Kimya was moving from one wall to another trembling like a fearful rabbit due to the fear of the first night. The shadow of her tiny body covered the ceiling under the candle night. She was anxious due to the infusion of women at the *dargah* concerning the first night. She did not know what to do and was walking in the room like a gazelle.

- You are probably tired! Sit down if you please.

- ...

- Do you have *wudu*?

- Yes.
- Forget about the customs. There is no prayer like *zifaf* (the first night) prayer. And there will be no interaction between us today. Let us pray the night prayer and you can sleep in the bed.
- How about you?
- I will recite Quran. If I need to sleep, the mattress by the door is enough for me.
- Don't you think that my father would be sad if he hears you slept by the door?
- If we do not tell anything, he will not be sad. After praying together, I said, "Have a good sleep". I blew the candle out and recited Quran by the window under moonlight.

The room in which we lived with Kimya was looking out into the courtyard of the madrasa. This small *madrasa* where Mawlana and his family resided served all of us and the whole family resided there together.

Kimya kept silent when required and spoke if she needed to speak. She grew in my heart with her morality, carefully chosen words. She never ceased to show her respect. She liked to talk with me. She was like a bird that was kept in a cage for years and needed to be listened to. The women in the *dargah* had kept her silent saying "Women should speak less or they shouldn't speak at all".

Kimya became a sage on the way of divine love day by day. One day she said,

- Is sight important for love?
- Of course.

- Then we will attain the Beauty of Allah within divine love, won't we?
- Love begins in sight; it is the sight not to see that unveils the mystery. The ladies who saw Joseph cut only their fingers at the first glance. If Joseph's love had entered their hearts at first glance, would not they cut their entire bodies?
- Are our souls unaware of the love of Divine beauty they saw at the realm of souls?
- Not every soul is unaware. Those who buried the mystery into forgetfulness would not see. Only the ones that unveiled the mystery would attain that sight.
- The mystery of the rose and rosebud?
- It is supposed that "Some will be rosebuds in the rose garden" and "some would be thorns of the rosebud".

Following the first days, the fearful Kimya became a completely different one who behaved like a talkative and childish girl. The women at the *dargah* were surprised by Kimya's behaviors. They bet whether she would not endure or commit suicide. Contrary to their expectations, her happiness made everyone surprised. They tried to understand what was happening to her. The public heard that Kimya improved in the science of state weeks later and surprised the women at the *dargah* by her talks on knowledge and wisdom. They began to envy her. When Kimya said, "You don't know Shams and all of us know him in a wrong way. I taste such a different spiritually with him that I do not want him to leave me the whole day. I cannot show patience when he prays the canonical prayers; I just want him to finish and go on with his speeches", they could not believe their ears.

Mawlana's younger son Alaaddin Chalabi was a few years younger than Sultan Walad. This unconstrained son would enter the madrasa together with his friends, which made me feel sorry. One day he passed by our room that opened to the courtyard. I warned Alaaddin Chalabi:

- Oh the light of my eyes…you are adorned with exoteric and esoteric morality but you need to be careful while passing by my window and room. The young Alaaddin Chalabi was offended by my words and answered in a rough manner.

- Whose house are you talking about, oh shaykh?

After these words, the coldness between us became worse than before and he hurt me deeply. I thought of shouting aloud against his stubbornness. If it were not for Mawlana's sake, I would damage him with a single sight.

The group who did not like me and caused my departure from Konya at the beginning did not calm down completely. After returning to Konya, they were on the lurk despite their apologies and were looking for a chance. This time, they added a few preeminent scholars of the city among themselves. They also managed to include Alaaddin into that circle. The opposition group was becoming more crowded.

I was talking with the dervishes in the courtyard one day. Alaaddin interrupted with no permission:

- The *qutbs* (poles) of this world are my father and grandfather. You are seeking help from the flame of a candle; he tried to provoke me in doing so.

- Mawlana has pearls of divine knowledge. He never thinks whether his words would be helpful for someone or not; but I have spoken by divine inspiration since my childhood. I may put one into attraction, make him clever, or discipline him. Forget about my harshness, my words are like whips that train the naughty ones.

- You are destructive like the wind and sharp as a knife. What do you have in your words other than trouble?

- When Mawlana speaks, you listen to him like quiet cats. When I begin speaking, you are looking for chances to jump on me like violent lions. However, he says what I say. He speaks silently whereas I speak aloud. There is no difference; Mawlana follows me as an imitator; and what a good imitator he is. Alaaddin began grumbling. I went on without hesitation.

- A babbler is grumbling. Son, calm down. Everyone speaks from his or her own heart. You are full of blood like that in a slaughterhouse and your eyes are erupting lava. Come to my sea and I will calm you down.

He stood up in anger and began walking towards me. I also stood up and got ready to throw my staff at him. The dervishes stopped him and took him away. When the event was heard in the city, those who hated me provoked Alaaddin Chalabi saying,

- How dare he do this? A stranger came and did not allow a son to enter his father's house? This is something unheard. They were taking the advantage of his rawness. I feel sorry for ones without love and for those poor fools who follow the others' evil deeds. How weak they are! Alaaddin was one of these poor ones. He liked to talk with another's mouth. He was a heartless and insignificant young man. Do not listen to those who say Alaaddin was among those who killed me in the future. He did not even have courage to kill a hen.

Provocations and my marriage to Kimya caused Alaaddin to act like a wild dog, which was ready to attack me any moment. His eyes were full of hatred; but a dog ready to bite never shows its teeth.

He entered my councils without permission, interfering and did his best to provoke me. The intriguers were happy with this condition. I informed Mawlana about these incidents. I was waiting for the right time not to sadden him. I wanted him to learn the truth from me. He left the room without saying anything. He went to Sultan Walad directly,

- Now I understand our father Adam. On one hand, there was Abel and on the other hand, there was Cain: mildness and toughness. I understood Adam's pain. My wise Sultan Walad and rebellious Alaaddin. What should I do, son?
- *La tahzan* (do not grieve) father. Say Allah and all troubles would disappear. Alaaddin is at an age of ignorance and full of energy. He loves and obeys you. His harshness is because of the intriguers around him. I will talk to him in an appropriate manner. He would calm down, do not worry about this, dear father."

Sultan Walad was friendly and mild; he was a scholar as his father. I had liked him for along time. He had a completely different state. He was a son Mawlana deserved. He filled my heart with admiration not only by his service at the *dargah* but also with the respect and manners he showed while he was bringing me from Damascus. If I had had a son, I would have wished him to be just like Sultan Walad. He would always ask how my mood and health was wherever he saw me and wanted to learn if I needed anything. He would get permission to participate in my councils and listen to me carefully. I heard that he would take notes during my sermons. When he learnt that I heard about this situation, he came and apologized. I said, "That's OK, you can write it down. If I had wanted my speeches to be written down, I would have chosen you as my inscriber". Hearing this, he felt so happy that he kissed my cheeks as sheep kisses a lamb.

- That's enough son, my face became wet as if it had ablution by your lips.

He laughed and said

- Forgive me oh shaykh and then he left.

Sultan Walad went to find Alaaddin as he promised his father. He found him smoking a water pipe in a teashop. After a fast glance, he understood that they were vagabonds.

What are you doing here with these vagabonds? Your place is where one the good-hearted ones reside.

- Two scholars in one family are enough. I am unnecessary here.
- What unpleasant words are you uttering? Do not forget that you are Mawlana's son.
- What does my father find in Shams the madman?
- Oh my brother, how vague are your eyes. Shams has such a brilliance that the serenity of his luminosity cannot fit in the sky. And your words are so rusty; Shams speaks in such a manner that you think the Heaven is speaking.
- I do not need your sky or sun. I want to smell the darkness of hell.
- Are you smoking opium? What a tactless speaking is that. I am your elder brother and I have some certain rights over you. I see that these vagabonds are more valuable for you.
- You are intoxicated with Shams and I am drunk with opium. Does it make any difference?
- Woe on you! I have protected and defended you until now. But if you make my father and Shams sad anymore, you will find me defending them.
- Send my belongings here; I will not come to the *dargah* anymore. Enjoy your Shams!
- Don't you care about my father?
- Does he think anything other than Shams? He is busy with Shams every time. This man of Tabriz enchanted all of you. What made me sorrowful was Kimya who is under his glamor. She married that old man although she knew I loved her. I hate all women.

- How dare you speak about our sister like that? Shame on love and the beloved. How could you love your stepsister?
- The hearts are in Allah's hand.
- Finding the truth is also in His Hands… May He lead you to the right way. You went astray; I cant do anything except pray for you. Come and take your belongings yourself.

Kimya loved stories and Persian poetry. She always wanted me to tell stories and read poems. As I read eastern stories and anecdotes, she listened to me with utmost care.

I told her the story of *Djamshid* and *Khurshid* once; she laughed so much that her voice was heard even outside the court. Kira Hatun and others were surprised.

During one of our conversations, I looked and smiled at her. She asked,

- Why did you smile, my dear Shams?
- When I see you, I remember the female lion of Sufism.
- Who is that female lion?
- Rabia al-Adawiyya. May Allah be pleased with her.
- My father told me her story when I was a child. And one day he looked at a Christian woman on the way home while from the bazaar and said three times "Rabia, Rabia, Rabia". The woman was surprised with the name he uttered. She searched the meaning of this name. She was surprised more when they said, "Probably Mawlana likened you to a Muslim *Saintess*, Rabia al-Adawiyya". Finally, she came to our *dargah* when she learnt about Rabia's life. All of us gathered in the courtyard thinking what she had to do with our father although she worked in indecent jobs. Then the Christian women went out with a Quran in her hands and covered her head with a scarf. We learnt from the dervishes that she met with the light of True Way while researching Rabia al-Adawiyya and decided to be Muslim. She confessed the Kalima-i Shahadah and told my father that she wanted to be

initiated by him. Following this event, the women at the *dargah* wondered about Rabia's life and wanted my father to teach them. My father said, "To be Rabia is not a task of desire but of love; not all hearts can endure to be Rabia. As I was trying to learn from the books, my father came and told me her story.

- I smiled because I saw the qualities of Rabia in you. You are brave as her.
- I want to listen to her features in your own words.
- Rabia al-Adawiyya was born in Basra; her father died when she was very young and she had to lead a life under poverty and misery of being an orphan.
- Allah is just. He takes something but he gives another thing on the other hand. This deprivation and poverty caused a sort of consciousness in the spirituality of Rabia who submitted herself to Allah; Rabia returned to her inner realm and soon was appreciated by the great saints of that period such as *Sufyan as- Thawri* and *Hasan al-Basri*.

Her belongings consisted of a mat in her small hut and a mattress filled with date leaves; but this did not make her sorrowful; on the contrary, it gave her peace and ecstasy.

As a master of fact, *Sufyan al-Thawri* came to visit her and offered, "Oh Rabia, your relatives may help you if you like; you can get rid of these humble mat and mattress and change your appearance"; however, Rabia gave a strict answer: "I do not complain about my condition and I do not need to demand anything. I did not appeal to the Owner of the world about my condition. Then I am unlikely to demand anything from those weak ones whose belongings don't even equal to a single atom in the world!"

Rabia had only one measure: it was to live this worldly life either in the most appropriate manner according to Islam or not. If one leads a life that is conformable to religious rules, that life attains its purpose according to her. It does not matter whether that life is lived on a mat or just on soil

One of the richest people of Basra, *Suleyman Hashimi*, wrote a letter to her and explained his wealth and the possessions, which would be even greater in the future. When he said, "All these are under your service; just accept me and my proposal", Rabia answered him severely: "Do not be arrogant about your wealth and do not trust it. It is like foam. It cannot prevent death or predestined thing that you are likely to live. Seek for what you will need before Allah and be consoled with it. And do not deceive yourself thinking that they will commit good with you wealth by declaring it in my will. Be your own guardian and spend your wealth on the way of Islam; thus fulfill it yourself. Do not forget that the things you mentioned in your letter that you are ready to sacrifice for my service would only burden and give darkness to my heart. They are far from me and are not desirable

The women demanded her advices when they visited her. The following is an advice given by her "Conceal your goodness just as you conceal your evil deeds. To claim goodness is like blowing flour against wind. The wind takes flour away and you lose it." Since Rabia devoted her entire being to faith and divine love, she did not think of marriage for this reason. They asked her why she had not married, she said, "Three things fill my entire world. So there is no time for thinking of marriage." They said, "What are those three things?" She said, "Will I pass away with faith? Will I be given my book from my right or left side? When the people are divided into two on the way of paradise and hell, where will I stand?"

- Do you have any anecdotes about her, Masters?
- Of course, I have. I will tell you about one of them. You will enjoy it.

One day a thief entered her house while Rabia was praying; she understood that the thief did not find anything. She said "Oh the poor man, just have ablution with the water in that ewer and pray two *rakah*s lest your efforts be in vain..."

The thief was overwhelmed with surprise and fear. He performed ablution and began praying. Then Rabia raised her hands and prayed.

"Oh lord, this poor man could not find anything in my house and I sent him to your gate. Certainly you are not like me. You always bestow sustenance upon the needy."

When she heard that the thief began repenting after canonical prayer, she supplicated "Oh Lord, this man waited a few minutes before Your door and You accepted him immediately; but this poor one (I) was there for an entire life and I have not been accepted as such!" The Divine voice said from within her heart;

"Do not grieve, we accepted him for your sake!"

- I have not heard about this incident before. Thank you, oh master.
- Why?
- For honoring me by means of likening me to such a lover.
- This was not a compliment, dear Kimya, it was the truth. You are tired. You'd better sleep a little.
- Oh master, I want to sleep on your knees if you do not mind. Will I bother you if I sleep until prayer time?
- Of course not. Enjoy your sleep.

Kimya's chastity made even the angels envy. It was probably due to Mawlana's spiritual training. She was not an ordinary woman; she was a treasure far away from arrogance and caprice. Her excessive respect made me sometimes feel shame. I could not sleep and went out to the courtyard one night. When she woke up not to find me in the room, she rushed to the window and found me watching the stars. She came to me with a glass of linden tea:

- Thank you. That is kind of you.
- You're welcome. Serving you is mercy for me, Master.
- You'd better go inside and I will come soon.
- Don't you know that the room is a dungeon for me if you are not there?
- One who named you was right.
- Why?
- Because your kindness and morality destroy one's chemistry (kimya in Arabic). We laughed and went in.

Our marriage with Kimya added new chains to the chains of happiness at the *dargah.* Kimya made me happy with her friendship; and my happiness and stay in Konya made Mawlana happy; Mawlana's happiness made Kimya happy; Kimya's happiness made Kira Hatun happy and as a result all these made Mawlana happier more than everyone. Our marriage did not cause any chaos as the intriguers expected. On the other hand, the pot of wickedness was boiling and Alaaddin was full of anger whereas the *dargah* was full of peace like that of spring. The only thing that transformed spring into autumn was the sudden sickness of Kimya.

Kimya asked me about death in one of our conversations.

- How is death?
- Your question is so long but the answer is very short.
- I could not understand it.
- Death is love.
- I did not understand it again. Are love and death intertwined?
- Each soul is married to love. Death is not a separation but it is the first night of truth.
- What is the bliss in love and death?

I stood up. I held her hands and let her stand up, too!

- Open your right hand towards heavens and your left hand towards earth. Close your eyes and we will begin whirling together with the entire universe. Beware of opening your eyes. You should not see what comes down to your right hand from the heavens. You should not see what falls down from your left hand to the earth; perform only *sama*.

When *sama* (whirling) was over, I wanted her to open her eyes. When she opened her eyes, her skin turned white. Her heartbeats were echoing in the room.

- You asked me about death, did you understand it now?

Her voice was full of joy and the letters were full of a childish excitement.

- I understood.
- For the lover, opening and closing the eyes was enough. However, springs and summers passed by that moment. There were autumns full of grief and winters full of trouble. Love and death are momentarily. It is the moment of the moment. To love is to be resurrected in death; death is to find oneself in love and to attain unity, my dear Kimya.
- Who is the lover for you?
- For me, a lover should be a person that burns everywhere when he stands up; everywhere will be full of resurrections!..
- I wish I met you years ago.

Then she kissed my hand. My hand had never smelled such a lovely scent. She enjoyed my speeches so much that it was like the words that were expelled in her heart attained freedom when I spoke.

Oh my dear Kimya
Why do you rush towards death
As soon as you learn love?

The cold hoarfrost of winter covered the trees like curtains before it snowed. There was a pain inside me growing. My dear Kimya became sick suddenly. First fever, then delirium at night and finally severe pains as she became weak. Abscesses appeared on her neck and on her back a few days later. We took her to the physicians. But it was useless. The abscesses were spreading all over her body. During the nights I fell into in to grief when she moaned in pain. I was holding her head on my knees and supplicating for her. Her pains became lighter by my breath and she fell asleep. When the morning calls for prayers were recited, I prayed while sitting lest she would not wake up; the sickness and pains of Kimya, who was the trust of Allah and then Mawlana, made me sorrowful. I had heard before that there was a physician in Horasan who healed abscesses. I decided to take her to Horasan but it was a great distance and she would not endure the conditions. I sent someone to bring the physician to Konya. However, Kimya Hatun died when the physician was on the way.

This was the first time in my life that I experienced such a suffering. I have never felt such a pain. The moth that tore its cocoon flew away and the spring that gushes through the rocks dried. Her smell was everywhere; it was so fresh on my garments as if it came from the realm of tales and stayed there only a single moment. It was as if we buried Heaves under the earth, not Kimya. The dreary clouds were on the ground and it was raining towards the sky. If I knew that Kimya was compassionate as such and if I understood that her separation would cause abysses inside me, I would resist marriage at the beginning. To lose the paradise after experiencing it is the most indefinable pain in the world.

Kimya was my walking Paradise. She never hurt me even once within our six months companionship. She cared for me a lot. With her innocence, she let me taste the mercy I had not seen from my mother and the respect I had not seen among dervishes. It was as if she discovered the orphan inside me. She would put a blanket over me, prepare water for my ablution, and clean my face with a towel with her hands. The calmness in her voice was music to me. She never made a wry face not even once. Not all these were due to a sense of duty but it was obvious that she did so out of love. I felt shame because of her sincerity, kindness and serenity. She never mooned when she was sick in order not to grieve me. She was a beautiful woman who cared for me more than anyone else. She was a rose, the rose garden that made the sun smile. Now, how can the sun smile without Kimya?

There was a lined sky at the very night when we buried Kimya… There were clouds on earth... It was a dilemma between existence and non-existence! I was deprived of her smell and I was looking for her voice on the walls. I went to scratch the stones and punch the walls to let them give me her voice. It was the most sorrowful night in my whole life; it was a night that had no end and a night that was as if they piled all the rocks in the world on my chest. I was drowning. She used to be my breath. Now I can understand how he became *hamush* and took refuge in the shelter of silence. There remained only a lilac shirt at the end of the bed and a white pillow that had figures of birds and deep holes on it; a kilim on the ground which she knitted with her hands and light from her eyes. I am on a praying mat, exhausted, thoughtful and offended... crying. That's to say, an old man with a cold appearance that was equipped with the deep silence of the river which has snowy mountains. My hands were pale and my lips have turned to an unusual purple. Me and a dead room without Kimya. What shall I do? The pain of love is so deep and lunatic that one can regard pain as his "soul". I fell down from a cliff. The mountain was rolling behind me but it could not even fill the abysses I fell down.

The sound of water was heard over the fire that twisted on my forehead. I want to penetrate into the bosom of mountains with the solitude of a desert. What shall I do with the rose garden that does not smell Kimya? Where are you Kimya, my *Mihriban*? *Mihr* means love and mercy in Persian. It also means the sun. *Ban* means one who possesses something. Thus, *Mihriban* stands for one who transforms into love, one who breathes love. No one's beloved is Mihriban. This era is without the Mihriban. Our nights are deprived of Mihriban that is without the sun. When love becomes deprived of Mihriban, the people think that passions, entertainment and lust are love. Those who want to learn the chemistry (*Kimya*) of love should know this great woman who was Mawlana's Kimya and my Mihriban.

Oh Kimya... you burnt my chemistry. I was able to know only in a short span of a lost life. If I had known you before your father, I would make you the Mawlana of the world, not Jalal al-Din; but I am sorry. There is only one love in this heart and it belonged to your father. Now I am silent my dear Kimya without you. I cry loud; my tears flow into my brain. Even crying would cry without Kimya, I wish she were alive.

My departure from Konya made Mawlana keep silent. Being quiet was good for something that is worth keeping silent. I am silent now, for, you are not here. I did not know that silence would make the left side of my body cold this much, I was hopeless as a flower that fell down in winter; I was cold when you did not exist in the room. Maybe I will get used to your leaving which is the worst fact. I would forget all that I know; you will not come. I will keep silent in this room in which all your memories reflect in each corner.

Mawlana and Sultan Walad were trying to console me but it was useless. My pain is deep and it burns inside more than the pits of hell. Mawlana feared for the possibility of Shams' departure from Konya. I consoled him:

- Only death may take me from this place where Kimya's memory smells everywhere. As soon as the news concerning Kimya's death was heard in the city, those who envied me took the advantage of this event and began provoking Alaaddin:
- This poor girl died of grief. Whosoever may endure Shams?

They opened the gates of gossiping and malice. Sultan Walad heard about the gossips and came to calm me down. However, I was so sad:

- You see Sultan Walad, they started again! They want to separate me from Mawlana and agreed on this task: But I will get lost this time and no one will find any trace of me.
- Master, your existence here is more valuable than your absence for my father in this path of love. Did not you say, "It is necessary to die and extinct in love so that the real living may be possible"?

As to Alaaddin, he took all his belongings from the *dargah* and began living with his vagabond friends. It was said that he began drinking alcohol and wondered in the streets of Konya while shouting aloud. Mawlana became depressed hearing this. *Dargah* was like a place of refuge. The father and his son were trying to comfort me, as I was so sad due to

Kimya's loss. Sultan Walad and I were consoling Mawlana whose heart was hurt due to Alaaddin's disobedience.

All right, the majority of people in Konya did not like me at the beginning; but they did not hate me to the extent of killing. There were only a few jackals that opposed me. Following my departure, they realized my value due to my absence and the number of them became even fewer. The fanatics whose authority and fame was shaken lost their hopes from the so-called "young" dervishes because of the sympathy of people that inclined towards me. Due to their fear from Mawlana and the public reaction, they could not give a *fatwa* for my murder. They decided to find an assassin out of Konya but could not succeed in doing so. Those who provoked Alaaddin against me lowered their voices at that moment. I knew certainly that Alaaddin would not agree with any plot made to kill me. In fact, Alaaddin was a young and emotional man. However, his anger would easily be calmed down. I regarded his behaviors to be the result of his ignorance and young age.

He realized that he became the object of gossiping among the public, yet it was too late. He was influenced by the rebellious speeches of *Ahi Awran* who stayed in Konya for a short time; then Aladdin went to Kirsehir to be initiated by him. When he left Konya, I forgave him afterwards. After a few months of my martyrdom, Alaaddin was wounded during the rebel of *Ahi*s against Sultan Kilicarslan and died there. His dead body was brought to Konya; his father led the funeral prayer and he was buried at the *dargah*.

THE MARTYRDOM OF LOVE

Had not I be thrown into deep wells
How would I see the sun despite its darkness?
Was it possible to be Shams before submitting the soul to the beloved?

Seven doors, seven rooms, seven questions, seven hangmen... seven riders were riding into the darkness of night; the horses of those seven people were Arab horses. The seven horsemen were raising clouds of dust. Nobody understood their language and they spoke less. Ciphered words, sights, mimics made their reticent position even more mysterious. The seven horsemen arrived in Konya after riding for seven days and nights.

The black wings of the night covered the city that was covered with a white cloth of snow; as the people stayed home emptying the streets in order to get warm, the north wind was blowing towards the inn to destroy the gardens. The mane of seven horses caused winds worse than the Mongolian breath.

Despite the cold seven tough men soaked in sweat came into the inn. They entered like the whistle of death into Sekerciler Inn where Shams came to polish the diamond of love years ago. One of them spoke in incomprehensible Turkish:

- Is the man of Tabriz in Konya?

- Which man of Tabriz? There are people from seventy-two nations in Konya. There are many men from the Tabriz. Which one are you looking for?
- The shaykh. The man from Tabriz who does not have any possession except for his black coat.
- That must be the Shams (the sun) of Tabriz. He is at the *dargah*.
- May your sun sink; it will certainly decline.
- Are you drunk fellows?
- We are not; but you are intoxicated without drinking.
- Shams also uttered the same words.
- We know
- How many rooms are there in this inn?
- Nine rooms for the guests and one for my family.
- How many customers are there?
- It is winter; the rooms are empty…
- All right then; take your family away; we want nobody here. We will rent all the rooms for two days. You may take whatever you want from this moneybag. But do not come here for two days.
- How about cleaning and food?
- We are clean by birth. And we can cook our own food.

The innkeeper could not understand what was happening. He took a handful of gold coins from the moneybag and left without turning back…

It was foggy and there was such a thick layer of mist that it was not possible to see. Due to morning drowsiness, there was nobody in the street except for some children. The gate of the inn was knocked harshly a few times. The door was opened. It way the milk boy.

- Where is the innkeeper?
- He is not here for two days.
- What should I do with the milk now?
- Pour it in the river.

- I beg your pardon?
- How much do you earn in seven days?
- Two gold coins.
- Keep the milk with you. If I give three gold coins, will you take something to the *dargah*?
- Which *dargah* is it? There are many *dargah*s in Konya.
- The one in which Shams of Tabriz resides; have you heard about him?
- Everybody knows him here.
- Wait a minute then.

The stranger brought something covered with a piece of red cloth and said,

- Take this and give it to Shams, right? Do not open it and do not tell anyone else.
- Right. Now give me the three gold coins.

I never abstained its troubles
And never submitted the suffering from you, oh love.
I speak of neither paradise nor hardship; I see neither attainment nor longing
I do not walk towards paradise; it runs towards me

The courtyard of the *dargah* was misty and it was empty due to the cold weather. A few dervishes were talking by a dry tree. The milk boy greeted them as he was holding the milk bucket. A dervish said,

- The kitchen (*matbah*) is over there.
- I did not come to the kitchen. I want to visit my master, Shams.
- First see *Atashbaz* effendi; he will tell where Shams is.

Atashbaz was stirring something in a huge pot with a big ladle. He was leaning left and right, and reciting verses from the Quran at the same time. When the milk boy entered the kitchen, Atashbaz took his fingers to his lips, which meant keep silent. The boy waited for some time… he waited almost half an hour standing. Atashbaz said,

- Tell me what you want.
- I wanted to see Shaykh Shams of Tabriz.
- Why, why do you want my Master?
- I brought a trust for him.
- What do you have except for milk? And my master does not like milk at all!

- An old man in Sekerciler Inn asked a question. He said, "Only Shams of Tabriz knows the answer; go and find out"

- It is all right then; he is downstairs, in the cellar. Be careful, it is dark inside; do not fall down there.

The milk boy entered in through the cold narrow passage and went down; as he was going down, the drops of sweat on his forehead dropped on to his face as cold as ice. He opened the cellar door. Inside the dark and cold room, there were vegetables in baskets, bunches of grapes hanging from the ceiling and melons, watermelons on straw… there was a man sitting on his knees contemplating in a corner.

- What are you doing here?
- Well, …
- Tell it and leave here at once.
- I brought a trust for you. Trembling, he gave the trust covered with red cloth.
- All right. You may go out. Leave this place immediately.

Shams removed the cloth and there was an extraordinary stone. It was Afgani stone that cuts glass and the soul as well. It was brown and shaped like a triangle. It was used by *Hashashi*s (disciples of Hasan Sabbah; it is believed that the word *assassin* was derived from this word-t.n) as a massage for whom they would kill. He took the paper and went upstairs. He said to Atashbaz:

- Stroke this paper with your palm.

A Persian word appeared on the paper where Atashbaz stroke. *Paranda* (the flying one; epithet of Shams-t.n). It was written seven times on the paper by milk…

Atashbaz was surprised seeing all these. When Shams threw the stone into the oven, the small brown stone extinguished the fire. Shams left the kitchen and caught one of the dervishes in the courtyard. He whispered something in his ear. The dervish left the *dargah* in a hurry.

It was almost the noon prayer time. Some people were walking towards the mosque… The dervish who was walking in a hurry was greeting everyone passing by and those sitting in front of the shops saying "*Hu Hamush Hu…*" He came to the inn. The door was knocked and it was opened… the dervish whispered in the ears of the man who opened the door, "Prepare seven questions in seven rooms". The one whom you expect will come here after the Morning Prayer…

Since my childhood I asked a question to all dervishes I met during conversations. The ones who heard my question would think that it belonged to a madman. However, the questions were of saints. Only the saints could answer them. What shall I do if the public did not know the difference between a saint (*wali*) and a madman (*dali*)?

This time, my questions were addressed to me. My trials were directed to me like a boomerang. I passed many tests and answered many questions. I hand only one more trial: which was to be beheaded. I would give my head as a compensation for love with love.

I wanted seven different questions. There had to be a dervish in each cell. Each of them would ask a question. The questions of seven doors were like a dragon with seven heads. The dervishes who learnt my demands discussed their questions for a long time and waited for me after preparing the most critical questions according to them.

I entered the first room. The dervish asked:

- Bayazid Bistami did not eat melons for sixty years. They asked, "Why don't you eat melons?" he said, "I do not eat melons, for, I do not know how Mohammed (P.B.U.H) ate it." what do you think about this answer?

I said,

- How can Bistami, who does not know how this melon would be peeled, possess even more mysterious and difficult knowledge? How can he inform us about them?

The dervish bowed down. He went out and jumped into the pond at the courtyard with his garments.

In the second room:

- Who is Satan?

I said,

- You are; for, we immersed in *Idris (Enoch)* for the time being. If you are not Satan, then why did not you drown in Idris? If you have anything from *Idris*, then why do you fear Satan? The dervish ran away shouting and tearing his garments.

In the third room,

- What's your sect? Why did you rebel against your essential nature? I said,

- Lovers do not belong to any sect nor do they have any way. I do not care about the jurists. I do not know anyone except for Mawlana who is the Imam of Love and I do not obey anyone. My aim is to be sacrificed for love. You are the ones who converted to other beliefs. The dervish took the Quran on the wall and kissed it. Then he left the room.

In the fourth room:

- What is unity?

I said, "to ask such a question to a shaykh is wrong and forgetfulness. One who knows his existence via suffering knows his Lord with loyalty; one who knows his existence via faults, knows his Lord via blessing. The dervish fainted there.

In the fifth room:

- Isn't *sama* unlawful?

Sama is the manifestation of Allah. It is the journey from this lower world to the supreme realm. It is lawful for ones who know and lawful for those who do not know. You should not pronounce *sama*, not to speak of performing it, oh ignorant one! The skin of the dervish turned pale and he left the room crying.

In the sixth room:

- Man is the only creature that claims servitude. What is the distinction between them?

I said, "Allah says 'I created man by My *Jamal* (Beauty) and *Jalal* (Majesty)'. In some people, only the *Jamal* manifests and he says 'I am a servant'. He says, "I could not know you as you deserve" like the Prophet (P.B.U.H.). Man is quite important in that he is the locus of manifestation of both Majesty and Beauty. Allah wants servants who unite Majesty and Beauty and covers Majesty by Beauty; He also wants those who are like Him. He calls them as perfect men. He wants servants of good nature and who possess perfectness by covering Wrath by His Mercy.

The dervish drew his sword and began walking towards me. His hands were trembling. He touched my beard with his sword. He wanted me to look into his eyes. When I cast my sight, he began crying terribly. He stroke his sword on the wall saying The Supreme Name aloud "*Allaah*"; he fainted there. The sound of the sword on the wall echoed firstly in that room and then in the entire building. All of the dervishes came and saw their friend fainted on the ground; they felt relieved.

The last door and the last question…When I entered in the seventh door, there was a dervish greater than the previous ones whose eyebrows were thick and his eyes were as black as tar. He was sitting cross-legged in one corner and cleaning his teeth with a dagger:

- Come on in Tabrizi. Since you cluttered my friends by your answers, it is certain that you are not an ordinary man. You know from where and why we come. Why do you live lazily instead of serving our organization like your grandfather?
- I prefer being mud in the streets of Konya than being raiders like you.
- You say you would be mud for Konya but vagabonds in Konya do not like you. We heard that they were looking for assassins from surrounding cities to kill you. We came here before allowing them to do so.
- They know nothing other than dry speeches. Now I wonder if you remember your tactlessness against our Shaykh when you left Konya and returned to Tabriz.
- Do you call that descendant of Satan a 'shaykh'?
- Then why did you escape from Tabriz to Damascus?
- I did not escape; I only followed the scent of my beloved.
- Then why did you come here from Damascus?
- To enable my *Hamush* to speak.
- You mean Mawlana?
- Do you ask the lover about love?
- What is your compensation for love?
- My head.
- Are you ready to give it?
- Of course I am.
- Then let us go out to the courtyard.

- I have a last wish.
- What is it? Do you want forgiveness? If you like, we may forgive your head on one condition. It does not matter, either you or Mawlana.
- Never… is my heart not contented with a single atom to make his hair dirty, not to speak of getting into a trouble. Finish your task with me without touching him or his family and go away to Tabriz.
- Then what is your last wish?
- Allow me to make my farewells to my *Hamush*.
- Will you escape?
- Do I seem like that? The lovers rush towards death. If I feared death, would not I escape before when I had a chance to go away?
- All right, we are waiting for execution of love at night.

The lover is one who gives Allah the trust of love that he took from him
Everything is sacrificed for supreme love within the path of love

The call for evening prayer was recited at an unusual time compared with the previous evenings in Konya. There were no birds at the fountains for they feared the silence of the steps of death. The city was silent as if it heard the news of the murder. There was not such gloominess on the streets even before the Mongolian invasion. The smoke from the chimneys was rising in a different way. There were no stars in the sky and the Pleiades was preparing themselves for the mourning of sun. The dervishes at the *dargah* had the feeling of ill will but they could not understand why... All the dervishes kept silent and it was as if all of them heard the same news and they became dumb. There was a smell of death in the air... The sky was irritable... the earth uncouth... The wind coarse... There was as if a mysterious power which drowns the cold weather that freezes the blood. It was 5th December.

Mawlana felt depressed all day and could hardly wait for Shams to pray the evening prayer. He did not pray in congregation. He waited for the beloved, *Hamush*. He did not know that his friend would be a pierced body for the sake of his love. The dervish told Mawlana that a milk boy came there and a dervish was sent to the bazaar by Shams. All these were quite unusual for Shams. He was anxious, what was happening? Did he leave Konya again forever? He wondered and went out of the *dargah*. He had a fine shirt on him… He was cold and his lips were trembling… The dervishes informed Sultan Walad about the incident. He came to his father immediately. He put the cloth he brought on Mawlana's back. He also feared that Shams might leave Konya. He could not pronounce his Fear lest his father might panic. Shams said a few days ago

- I am exhausted… One day I could disappear and even the messengers of doomsday would not find me"

The silhouette of Shams appeared far away as a shadow through the fog. He was coming but he seemed tired. It was as if he walked four days without resting… He embraced Mawlana. Mawlana was trembling by the shocking of this embracing. Mawlana was ready to utter something when Shams raised his fingers to his lips to mean keep silent. They went to another room to perform prayer. When Mawlana was holding Shams' arm for leading the prayer, Shams held his hands and said,

- The leader (*imam*) of love is also the leader of our prayer. They began praying as Mawlana was the *imam*, Sultan Walad and Shams were in congregation. This canonical prayer was so important for Shams; for, this would be the last prayer of them with Mawlana. Canonical prayer was "the light for eyes" according to Prophet Mohammad. Shams whispered: "what a bliss to pray canonical prayer that is light for eyes together with Mawlana who is the light of my heart". After the prayer, Mawlana said,

- You must be hungry, but Atashbaz is not here. Let me prepare food for you. Let us cook *halwa*. You seem weak, it may help you to. Why are you so pale?

- Probably I am cold; don't worry, I will recover. Maybe you will eat my *halwa* sometime during the night. I want to be alone with you, my dear *Hamush*. Is it possible to do so, my dear son Sultan Walad? Sultan walad asked for permission and left the room. Shams put his head on his Hamush's knees. They remained still for about half an hour. Then Shams told Mawlana what had happened. The friend began crying but Shams tried to console him.

- I supplicated my Lord in Damascus and wanted a mirror to watch my love. My Lord bestowed you upon me and I watched you.

- Do not go…

- Don't worry, it's time to keep the promise.

- What promise?

- I prayed to my Lord to bestow you. My Lord said, "What would you do if I bestow the mirror?" I said, "My head" without hesitation. I devoted my head for love. That was the promise.

- Mawlana was crying and was about to faint. His lips, hands, and all his organs were trembling.

- Do not cry my dear friend! Your voice should not be heard. Do not make the residents of *dargah* worried. You should understand it. Is there another way other than going?

- Do you remember Caliph Othman's martyrdom? Let me tell you dear Mawlana.

You know, the rebels came to Medina for a sudden raid. They would slaughter people for the sake of Allah. It was alleged to fight for God's sake in a holy city. They came from three Muslim cities in three groups. Their intention was obvious: to kill Othman. The people of Medina were watching. Only Ali and his children were protecting him. Ali came to Othman one evening.

- Oh, Othman… Allow me to defeat these raiders.

- No Ali, I do not want people to say, "Othman shed blood in the city of the Prophet" about me.

- However, they will shed your blood. Why don't you allow me though you know their intention?

- Ali sit down and listen to me.

After performing the evening prayer, I sat leaning on the wall. I fell asleep. In my dream, there was a dining table in this room. The Holy Prophet was sitting at the table. Abu Bakr was sitting on the right and Umar was sitting on his left. There was only a bowl of soup. They were waiting as if they were waiting for someone's coming before beginning to eat. Then I entered the room. The Holy Prophet smiled and said,

- Oh Othman, where have you been? We were waiting for you. Then I woke up and understood that I will be a martyr. Now tell me Ali, is it true to let the lovers wait long?

Then Othman became a martyr for the compensation of love although he knew the results. Now, it is my turn my dear Mawlana. Now, oh my *Hamush*... Even love has compensation. If he had willed, Othman would have saved his body; how about his soul? Give me permission my dear Mohammad. This is our last meal and this is the last glass of water. You will say that dessert is missing. You will eat *halwa*; how will halwa taste sweet together with the pain of separation?...

Mawlana did not want his friend to go out. For, the result was obvious. It was known and predestined. Mawlana said to his *sun* "don't" silently. Mawlana raised his voice,

- Don't, don't go, Shams.

- Let me go, I cannot sleep; for my soul is intoxicated with love; cover my body with the leaves of jasmine and rose; read me what death wrote on my forehead by its hands.

Cover my heart that became pale with the sound of the *nay* and *qudum* by a piece of cloth.

Mawlana began crying. Shams said,

- Remove your tears; do not take me to a crowded graveyard so that my sleep would not be dispersed by the sounds of clinking skulls and bones. Take my body to your *dargah* so that the shadows might come and sit near at dawn. Bury me deep and cover my body with soft soil, put some rose and lilacs on me… They would release the good scents of my heart into the air; they would unveil the mystery of my inner peace even to the sun. Leave me to Allah and go away slowly, leave me in peace.

Mawlana was still… Time was still… Space was still…Shams disappeared spreading the veils of darkness as his eyes spoke smiling "there is no farewell in the station of lovers; we never departed…."

Everybody is beautiful and meaningful in his or her appropriate time
There is no sense in living that very moment after losing it
Now go…
Do not violate the tradition and customs of love, and the course of the beloved

Shams left the *dargah* without waiting for the call for *ish'a* (the prayer following the evening prayer-t.n.). It was raining. Shams was walking towards the Sekerciler Inn through narrow streets and stone paths. There was a garden surrounded by abandoned houses between the *madrasa* and the inn. He stopped there hearing a strange sound. It was a small puppy. He followed the sound and saw a female dog under a collapsed wall. Shams removed the bricks and earth on the dog. He caressed the dog and its puppy. The puppy was hungry. Then he went out to the street and knocked the first door. An old woman opened the door. He wanted some bread and milk. The woman thought he was a beggar. She brought some milk and bread at once. Shams placed the dog and the puppy in a safe place in the garden, began walking fast to the inn thinking that he was late. In the meantime, he saw a huge well with an opening in the garden and remembered the story of Prophet Joseph. "Our Master Joseph fit in the well but people in the world do not fit in it now". Then he whispered, "Lord, make this well my grave".

He was near the Inn. When he arrived there, the speed of the rain increased. He knocked at the door. As he was waiting at the door, he prayed, "oh death, cover me with your white wings; for, my friends do not need me. Oh death, embrace me with full love and mercy; let your lips touch mine, which never tasted the kiss of a mother, which never touched the cheek of a sister and kiss the fingertips of the beloved... Come and take me, oh dear death".

The door of the inn was opened slowly. The garments of Shams were entirely wet. He greeted and entered into the courtyard. He came near to the small pond in the middle of the courtyard.

There was candlelight in one room. It was then blown out. There was nothing in the darkness except for shining seven swords. The brightness of the swords was dazzling like streak of lightning in the blinding darkness.

Six dervishes were standing in a circle. The seventh dervish said,

- Our shaykh wonders something about you. Will you answer it?

- You may ask it.

- Why did you leave the Mongolian commander alive although you had a chance to kill him? Don't you know that you betrayed your ancestors?

- I hated disgusting politics throughout my whole life. I never washed myself with the Satan's water neither in the past nor now.

It was these children of Satan who murdered caliph Othman. Isn't that breath of Satan, which killed Husain in Karbala? I have nothing to do with Mongolians; Allah bestows sainthood to whom he chooses and the troubles to one who deserves it. Woe on you! You think that you fight for God's sake. May my blood be lawful for love and unlawful for you. Oh the sons of Hasan Sabbah! What's the difference between you and the hyenas of Yazid? Shame of your splendid garments and the staff you carry. Shame of love!

- What is your last wish?

- Let me write a few words. Would you send it when you leave this place tomorrow? And I haven't prayed the night prayer. I want to be killed during canonical prayer just like our Master Imam Ali…

Shams had his ablution with the water from the pond. His black coat was wet. Shams spread the coat on the wet ground as a prayer mat. He completed the *sunnah* part and started the *fardh*. He said, "Allah is the Greatest" and began reciting Quran aloud. In the first *rak'ah*, he recited *sura al-Shams* after *al-Fatiha*. One of the dervishes began crying. They realized that all the dervishes would be relented if they let him continue as such. The chief dervish stroke his knife on the back of Shams. Shams was still standing… the second one.. Third... The fourth… The fifth… The sixth… Shams fell down on the stoneground. He tried to stand up but fell aside. As he was trying to stand again, he still was reciting *sura al-Shams*. Then he sat on his knees.

The seventh and the strongest stroke pierced into the back of his head and his neck fell towards the right. As the dervishes were waiting for his prostration, Shams whispered the following saying of the Prophet hoarsely, "*Allah also loves one who wants to attain Him*".

One of the dervishes kicked his back. Shams fell down on the stoneground again; his lips were bleeding and teeth fell out onto the ground. His black coat turned into red. The intention of the dervish who held his hair was to cut his head off.

The chief dervish prevented him. He said, "Let him give his last breath. Then throw him into the nearest well. Cover him with his own garments. Wash the ground. We will set off in the morning".

However, Shams was still alive. He raised his head slowly from the ground made of Sille stone and said, "*Allah is the best friend. Lord! I love You and submit my soul as a present*"...

Oh Love! You are such a person that
The full ones of the world are the hungry ones of your attainment.

Mawlana whispered something with a tearful voice into the ears of Sultan Walad. The cheeks of Sultan Walad turned into red and his eyes were wide open. He put his hand on his father's shoulder. Mawlana was trembling. He was trembling. Father and the son cried for a while…

The door was knocked. It was knocked again. It was knocked for the third time and Mawlana said,

- Come in.

One of the dervishes, Bilal, wanted permission and entered in. Mawlana, who covered his eyes with his hands could only say, "yes, my dear Bilal" tearfully.

Sultan Walad stood up and went to the well his father mentioned with two other dervishes. They walked as they were reciting the verses of Quran. They stopped. Finally, they recited *sura al-Fatiha* and raised their hands to their faces, which means "Amin". Sultan Walad thrust out his hand and said,

- Bilal and Hamdha! Tell me your allegiance.

The two dervishes were surprised. What was the allegiance during the nighttime? What initiation was it?

- Put your hands on mine and swear not to unveil our secret even if you have to give your head.

The dervishes were surprised… What was happening? What secret? They put their hands on the hand of Sultan Walad, "we swear by the beautiful Names of Allah. We swear over each letter of Divine Word. Whatever you say is welcome. Our loyalty is forever"

Sultan Walad hanged down a piece of rope into the well. He said to Bilal

- Go down and take our Master on your back. Bring him up.

It was foggy and the weather was extremely cold in Konya. There was no sound around. The barking of dogs were suppressed with the rustling of leaves. The dogs already smelt the corpse in the well; however, the ones who killed Mawlana's Shams also guarded his body against wild animals. They understood that the ones coming there were Mawlana's son and the dervishes; so, they left that place quietly.

Atashbaz who was busy with cooking for the dervishes and training them at *chilahana* was old and tired. Mawlana did not want his father's trust, Atashbaz, to be more tired. Mawlana told him to settle in a small house in Meram. Mawlana said,

- Oh my friend who plays with the fire… You have exerted such a great effort for me that I want to give you this house as a gift. Now it is time to rest.

- But Shaykh, I cannot leave you. How can I live without your smell and breath?

- I know. Do you think that I would not miss your *tirit* and the other dishes? I like Meram. I will visit you in spring and summer. We will fill both our hearts and stomach.

Atashbaz was consented with the decision and was sent to the house in Meram. He was relaxing in this house with a single room which was situated in a silent setting amongst the songs of nightingales and growing roses, which Mawlana liked much.

An equestrian was riding through the darkness from the *dargah* to the gardens of Meram. The horse was tired and the rider was in a hurry as they arrived in the isolated house in Meram surrounded by poplar trees. The house was consisted of a single room and the fire in the stove was almost extinct. The door was knocked. The door opened with creaking. The one who opened the door recognized the rider and greeted him saying, "*Hû*". The heads leaned to the right and then to the front (a way of greeting among Mawlawis-t.n.)... The rider gave a piece of cloth and the landlord smelled it.

- Our master wanted you to cook *halwa* but not with the flour used in normal circumstances. He wants you to cook with earth and recite *sura al-Takathur* until you finish cooking.

- *Aiwallah...Aiwallah...* The thing he wanted would be ready until he comes here. Will you return now?

- No, I will prepare a grave.

- Aye, *Amanna.*

As he was cooking the *halwa*, Mawlana was on the way to Meram; Sultan Walad and the two dervishes carried the body on their backs and brought it to the garden. When they arrived there, they heard the sound of the *nay* and stopped suddenly.

Mawlana came there alone. He was sitting cross-legged and playing the *nay* (reed) at the isolated place where Shams wanted to come very much but never could.

This was the first time Sultan Walad saw his father blowing the Reed and it was the first time he heard these tunes.

"Oh the master of love, do not think that you left

Do not think that you extinguish the fire inside me"

Sultan Walad and the dervishes put the body on a large stone slowly which was covered with his own blooded garments. In the meantime, Mawlana came forth crying, "Oh Shams, which heart can endure this condition, which eyes can look at you? Woe on me! When he came nearer to the dead body, he staggered; but his son and the dervishes prevented him from falling down. He cried and cried continuously... He cried so much that it was as if the thunders accompanied Mawlana's mourning.

Sultan Walad, who did not like his father's condition and felt grief said,

- Oh father, do you want them to boil water?

- Son, the martyrs are buried without being washed and shrouded. Allow me to smell the friend for the last time.

Then he caressed Shams' head that was covered with blood and smelled his beard. He cleaned the blood on his face with his fingers; he smelled Shams' face and kissed him. The vehemence of his crying increased.

- Which cursed hands stroke their swords, my dear Shams? Which remorseless ones covered your gentle body with blood? Even the angels in the sky felt shame for this great sin on earth. Oh, my Paranda! Was it written in your destiny to fly in blood? My dear Shams... Where did you go leaving me here? I wish I could separate the veins of night and take you in my bosom again. I wish I could put my head on your knees". With his father's head on his shoulder Sultan Walad tried to tranquilize his fathers pain and silently ordered one of the dervishes to recite the call for the funeral (*sala*).

The dervishes recited the call for funeral. The friend (*Mawlana*) stood up and glorified Allah to commence the prayer. They began praying the funeral prayer at night. Shams was the second one whose funeral was performed at night after Caliph Othman throughout the history of Islam.

After the prayer, Mawlana embraced his friend's body and put it into the grave.

He hardly spilt some earth over it. He crouched there and began reciting the verses of Quran. Sultan Walad, Atashbaz and other dervishes were busy filling the grave with earth.

"If the sky would hear the separation and understand it,

Its stars would cry as well as the sun and the moon.

If the Sultan knew from which throne he would be abdicated

He would also cry as well as his crown and throne

If the flying bird knew why it was hunting

Its wings would be broken and it would start crying

The ears of the end of the life would not hear the screams

Would it endure the rain of blooded heart?

The world is an enormous mother that eats its own child"

Dear friends, our thrust is our guest here until everything settles down; then you may bring him to our home. The station of Shams is our *dargah*. Sultan Walad! No one should unveil our secret and my will is that you should bury me next to my friend in our *dargah*.

"I kept silence. I remained silent, as it is due by showing patience! There is a scream bleeding in the depthness of my heart; I did not open my heart to everyone... I stroke the knife to myself and I became quite..."

The dry frost made the blood frozen the following morning. Konya was like an abandoned the city. A city whose night smells death has a daytime that is silent as the Last Day. The door of the *dargah* was knocked. An old man wanted permission to enter in. He wanted to see Mawlana. Mawlana was sitting in the smallest cell in the corner of *dargah* with a silence of death. Sultan Walad and Kira Hatun were worried about him and they were standing there as if they were guarding him. The dervish told Sultan Walad that an old man brought a valuable trust for Mawlana. Sultan Walad wanted them to control the garments of the old fellow. They did not find anything except for an emerald handkerchief he held firmly in his hands. Sultan Walad remembered this handkerchief from somewhere but could not recall where. Then Mawlana came out crying,

- I felt his smell; he came. Look, Shams is not dead… Our *dargah* is smelling with his perfume. Mawlana took the handkerchief suddenly and smelled it.

- This handkerchief belongs to Shams. Tell me where he is and I will give you all that I have for your good news.

- Dear father, gain your conscious; it is only a piece of cloth.

He whispered in Mawlana's ears, "don't you remember, we buried him last night".

The old man who brought the handkerchief said,

- Master, some strangers whom I have not seen before wanted me to bring this handkerchief to you.

Mawlana entered in and smelled it. He opened it fearfully. There was a note written on a yellow piece of paper:

"I seek for you my dear Mawlana even if they cut off my head and throw it into a dark well… They let my blood come out from the jugular vein... Send the pieces of my body to nine different countries… Even if several herds of jackals attack my body… The pains would not let me stop although they would tire me; You're my essence, I search for you with your very essence, my dear Mawlana. By Allah, I wish my death would be before your eyes so that you might see what dying for love means".

Mawlana fainted thereof.

BIBLIOGRAPHY

1. Anbarcioglu, M.Ulker; Sultan Veled, Maarif.
2. Askin Halleri, Sufi Kitap.
3. Barks Coleman, Mevlana. Dogan Kitap.
4. Baytur, M. Bahari; Divan-i Kebir.
5. Bekiroglu, Nazan; Cumle Kapisi, Timas Yayinlari.
6. Can, Sefik; Mesnevi, Kultur Bakanligi Yayinlari.
7. Cetinkaya, Bayram Ali; Şems-Mevlâna Dostlugu, Insan Yayinlari.
8. Eflaki, Ahmed; Ariflerin Menkibeleri, Kabalci Yayinlari.
9. Gencosman, M.Nuri; Şems-i Tebrizi, Makalat, Atac Yayinlari.
10. Golpinarli, Abdulbaki; Mevlâna Celaleddin.
11. Kabakli, Ahmet; Mevlâna, T.E.V. Yayinlari.
12. Rifai, Kenan; Mesnevi Serif, Kubbealti Yayinlari.
13. Schimmel, Annemarie; Islam'in Mistik Boyutlari, Kabalci Yayinlari.
14. Schimmel, Annemarie; Tanrinin Yeryuzundeki Isaretleri, Kabalci Yayinlari.
15. Sah, Idris; Sufinin Yolu, Dogan Kitap.
16. Turkmen, Erhan; Şems-i Tebrizi'nin Ögretileri.
17. Urkmez, Melahat; Sems Tebrizi.
18. Yagmur, Sinan; Tennure ve Ates, Esra Yayinlari.
19. Yeniterzi, Emine; Tasavvufun Kitabi.
20. Watts, Nigel; Sevginin Yolu, Samsara Yayinlari.

TANNURA AND FIRE

MAWLANA JALA AL-DIN RUMI

By SINAN YAGMUR

- Why did Rumi married twice?
- Were Rumi and Hodja Nasr al-Din enemies?
- Did Rumi organize the murder of his youngest son Alaaddin?
- Did he participate in his funeral prayer?
- Is it lawful to throw coins into the wishing well?
- Did Rumi poison Ahi Awran Wali?
- Is Rumi a spiritual master or a Saint?
- What caused Rumi's depression?
- Was Shams killed or did he die naturally?
- Are there any contradictions In His Mathnawi from the point of Sharia?
- Is Rumi a traditionist? Why does he love Konya?

Tannura and Fire not only gives answers to these questions but also is a reference book due to its authenticity.

It is available in bookshops and online bookstores.

TEARS OF LOVE- II

MAWLANA JALA AL-DIN RUMI
A Biographical Novel

By SINAN YAGMUR

Rumi fainted all of a sudden.

He woke up at midnight wandering "Shams...Shams..." There stood only his son, Sultan Walad. He was crying as he was holding his father's hands. Rumi wanted them to open the walnut chest. Sultan Walad opened the blood-covered coat as he opened the chest. Mawlana Jalal al-Din Rumi smelled the coat and began crying. "Oh Shams, take me there, too. I am weak in your absence. Life is coarse. People are even coarser than the life". ..